Once upon a Felt Board

by
Roxane Chadwick

illustrated by Janet Skiles

Cover by Janet Skiles

Copyright © Good Apple, Inc., 1986

ISBN No. 0-86653-338-9

Printing No. 9876

GOOD APPLE, INC.
BOX 299
CARTHAGE, IL 62321-0299

Table of Contents

Chapter I

Preparing the Story

Tell "Hopper's Whoppers" to a first grade class; watch the children's eyes widen as the paper bag pops over the frightened mouse. A girl bites her fingernail as Hopper dashes into the tiger's cage at the zoo. As the tale ends, she sighs contentedly. That sigh and the smile that follows is the reward for preparing the story. Share a good story with a group of children. You'll both enjoy it.

This mutual pleasure is not an accident but a carefully calculated effect. Find a likeable story. Learn it well enough to relax and watch the children's reactions, instead of worrying about the sequence of the tale. Practice the motions on the flannel board. Keep a cheat sheet, text, and outline close by, just in case. Plan carefully and enjoy the story time along with your audience.

You need no special talents to tell a flannel board story. The flannelgraphs keep your hands busy. You can delight children with the stories that follow if you speak clearly and devote time to prepare the story. Storytellers come in all sizes, shapes, and personalities. Some have a dramatic approach; others quietly narrate a tale. Both methods and innumerable varients between succeed.

Children are accustomed to watching adventures that are broadcast impersonally over the television. Tell them a story face to face and they cherish it like a personalized gift. Children's receptivity makes the storyteller's job pleasant.

While the task is pleasant, sound preparation makes the story time successful. Children feel few social pressures to be polite and listen if they are bored. If they don't like a story, they will simply not listen. If the logic of the story is unclear because the storyteller forgot part of the tale, they will not listen. But if the story is well-prepared, the children will be caught up in the magical narrative bond that develops between storytellers and their audiences.

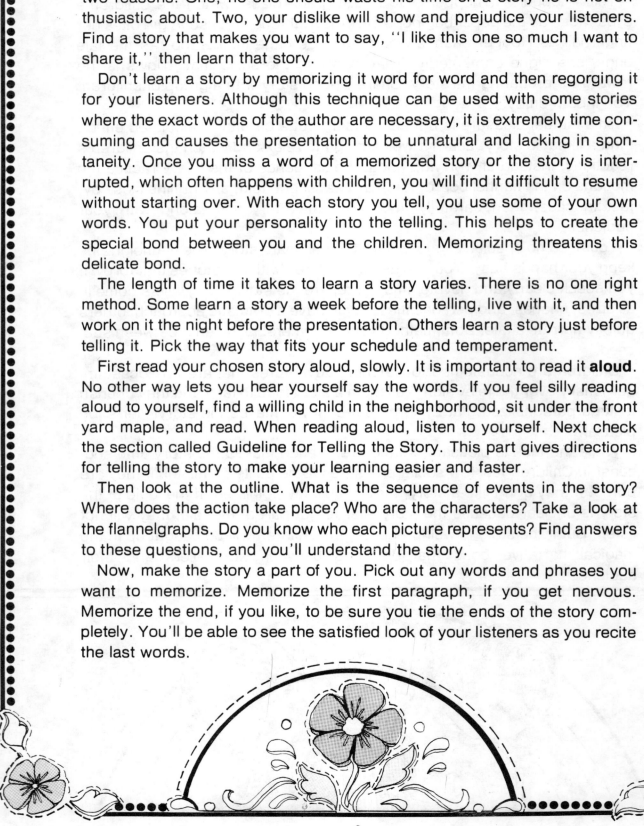

The first step is to find a story you like. If you dislike a story, don't tell it for two reasons. One, no one should waste his time on a story he is not enthusiastic about. Two, your dislike will show and prejudice your listeners. Find a story that makes you want to say, ''I like this one so much I want to share it,'' then learn that story.

Don't learn a story by memorizing it word for word and then regorging it for your listeners. Although this technique can be used with some stories where the exact words of the author are necessary, it is extremely time consuming and causes the presentation to be unnatural and lacking in spontaneity. Once you miss a word of a memorized story or the story is interrupted, which often happens with children, you will find it difficult to resume without starting over. With each story you tell, you use some of your own words. You put your personality into the telling. This helps to create the special bond between you and the children. Memorizing threatens this delicate bond.

The length of time it takes to learn a story varies. There is no one right method. Some learn a story a week before the telling, live with it, and then work on it the night before the presentation. Others learn a story just before telling it. Pick the way that fits your schedule and temperament.

First read your chosen story aloud, slowly. It is important to read it **aloud**. No other way lets you hear yourself say the words. If you feel silly reading aloud to yourself, find a willing child in the neighborhood, sit under the front yard maple, and read. When reading aloud, listen to yourself. Next check the section called Guideline for Telling the Story. This part gives directions for telling the story to make your learning easier and faster.

Then look at the outline. What is the sequence of events in the story? Where does the action take place? Who are the characters? Take a look at the flannelgraphs. Do you know who each picture represents? Find answers to these questions, and you'll understand the story.

Now, make the story a part of you. Pick out any words and phrases you want to memorize. Memorize the first paragraph, if you get nervous. Memorize the end, if you like, to be sure you tie the ends of the story completely. You'll be able to see the satisfied look of your listeners as you recite the last words.

Memorizing even small parts of a story are difficult for some people and easy for others. One method is the linear approach. Begin by learning the first phrase. Then look at the text and read aloud the next phrase. Put the text down and recite the first two phrases. Then read on, repeating the process until the whole paragraph is learned. With the linear approach, a glance at the first phrase prompts the whole paragraph to spill out.

The tape recorder method also works. Tape the parts to be learned. Play them repeatedly while you drive, cook, shower, or whatever chores you find monotonous. Play the tape before you sleep. And zap! The next morning, it's memorized. One caution, this method, which is similar to how children learn the words to a popular song, doesn't work for everyone. Other people find that writing the words helps. Do whatever method works for you.

The last step: practice telling it. Using the outline and the memorized beginning and ending paragraphs, try to tell the story without the felt characters. Discover any passage that is difficult for you. Mark it on your copy. Reread the section aloud. Reread the whole story aloud and try to tell it again.

Practice telling the story without the outline. Tell it to the mirror, **aloud**. Tell it to your dog. Dogs are excellent listeners.

Occasionally, a stubborn part of the story isn't learned and the deadline for telling the story has arrived. Resort to cheat sheets. It's the end product that counts. Type the difficult part on a piece of paper. Then read the difficult section when its time comes in the story. Be creative! Tape the cheat sheet on the back of the felt character that goes on the board next. Read the passage, then use the character. Cut a pumpkin from orange paper and tape the cheat sheet to it for a Halloween story. 3'' x 5'' cards work. Or highlight the section in the book.

So far, you have chosen a story, read it aloud, studied the outline, memorized the beginning and ending passages. You have practiced aloud with the outline, reread tricky sections aloud, and reread the whole story. You know the story. You've made your cheat sheets. Now, add the flannelgraphs.

Preparing the Flannelgraphs

The characters for the stories are provided for you. Color within the solid lines of the black and white drawings with marker. The broken lines around characters' faces make cutting easier. Light colors work best. Uncolored characters could be used, but full color attracts the children's eyes. Only a few extra minutes are needed to add color. Perhaps your students could color copies of the characters, and you could choose a ''winner's'' coloring to be used. A parent volunteer might color the characters.

Before coloring the characters, check the Felt Characters and Props List section. Some items must be a specific color. For example, in "Jon's New Year's Morning," it is essential for his fireman's hat to be silver so it can reflect the sun's rays. If items are not the "correct" colors, your audience will tell you.

After the characters are colored, cut along the outside lines either solid or broken. Glue felt or flannel to the back. Rubber cement works well and doesn't buckle. The flannelgraphs are now ready to help you tell the story.

Using the Flannel Board and Flannelgraphs

Get a flannel board. Most school supply stores sell them. A flannel board is easy to make if one is not available. A 2' x 3' piece of plywood or composition board can easily be covered with flannel. Tape, thumbtack, or staple a piece of flannel or felt to the board. Don't glue the flannel to the board because glue lessens the static electricity which causes the figures to adhere to the flannel. A neutral color is best for the background color: black, dark blue, light blue, or gray. White gets dirty quickly.

A small cork bulletin board with felt thumbtacked inside the frame works well. It has the advantages of having a frame that a handle can be screwed into for carrying and the felt can easily be changed to fit a story.

Choose a flannel board that is big enough (2' x 3'), stiff enough not to bend or sag so the characters won't fall off, and light enough to carry if you are a portable storyteller.

The second item needed is an easel or prop to hold the flannel board while you tell the story. Small table easels can be purchased at school supply centers. Collapsible ones are more portable. Leaning the board against a chair back is not completely satisfactory because the board can slip and come crashing down in the middle of a story.

A heavy cardboard box can be cut to make a satisfactory easel. Locate a box approximately 16" x 13" x 13". This is a standard book box that movers use for packing books. Any recently moved family should have some. If the top has been removed, the box can still be used. If the top is intact, fold the flaps inside for added support and durability.

Cut off the front (the longest side) leaving a 2-inch lip. (See Step 1.) In the middle of each side, cut down vertically to 3 inches from the bottom. From that point cut horizontally toward the front, leaving a 3-inch lip on the front half of the sides. (See Step 3.) Find a point on the 3-inch lip about 1 ½ inches from the vertical cut. At this point make a slit 1-inch deep into the lip. (See Step 4.) Now cut a second slit in the lip closer to the front of the box. The distance the second slit is from the first slit should be equal to the width of the edge of your flannel board plus ¾ inch for ease. Fold the tab formed by the two slits down inside the box. The easel is finished. (See Step 5.)

The felt board sits in the slots and leans against the vertical side pieces. The new easel can be painted, covered with Con-Tact paper, or used as it is.

Gather together the flannel board, easel, flannelgraphs, and any other props that are needed for the story. Position the characters in the order in which they appear. Read through the story. At each footnote turn back to the section Movements of the Felt Board Characters, read the instructions and follow the movements. After doing this once or twice, the movements will become easy because most of them are natural actions.

Storytelling with a flannel board is designed to stimulate children's imaginations and encourage an interest in oral language with a few visual props. Do not be concerned if you can't make the characters look like they are running or jumping. The children will fill in with their imaginations. In this way the children are active participants in the story.

Practice once more. You are ready to tell the story with the flannel characters. You will be great.

MAKING AN EASEL FROM A BOX

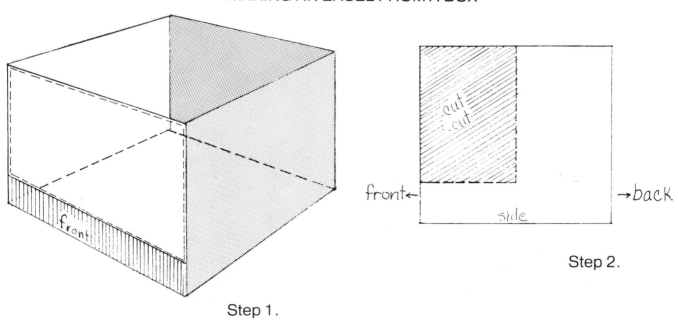

Step 1.

front← side →back

Step 2.

MAKING AN EASEL FROM A BOX

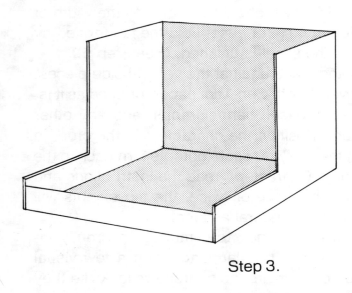

Step 3.

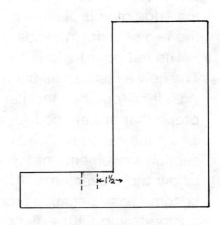

Step 4.

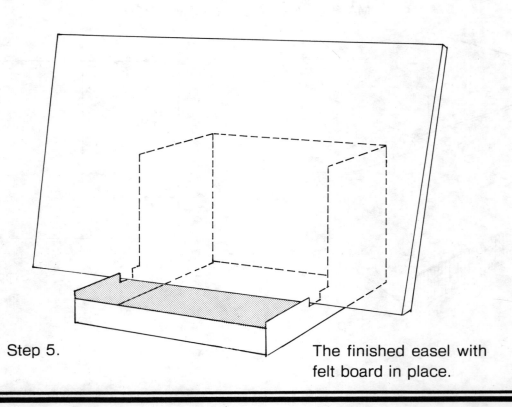

Step 5.

The finished easel with
felt board in place.

Setting Up

The work of preparing the story and gathering the equipment is over. You are ready to share your special gift of a story with some children. Find a place to tell the story where you will be comfortable. If the children have to sit on chairs, put the easel on a table in the front of the room. Stand or sit on a tall stool to tell the story. Right-handed people usually prefer the board on their left. If the children sit on the floor, which is preferable, prop the board on a chair or low table. This works fine with a group under twenty-five. With a larger group, stand with the board on a tall easel. A chair on top of a table could substitute for a tall easel. Be sure all children can see clearly. Beware of the ones who sit close and have to crane their necks to see. Children want to be close to the storyteller, but will enjoy it better if they are comfortable. Check with the children at the edges of the group to see if they can see before you begin the story.

During the setup time, find a moment to relax. Sometimes after hurrying to get to an appointment and set up correctly, tension creeps in. Take deep breaths, yawn, stretch, swallow, or hum to calm yourself.

Position the board, relax, arrange the felt characters in sequence behind the board or somewhere out of the children's sight. You are ready to begin.

Presenting the Story

Introduce yourself. Announce that you have a good story to share. Give any introductory remarks that are needed. Some stories have words that need to be defined for the youngest listeners or background information that might add to the children's enjoyment. They are listed in the section called Hints. The group you are telling the story to will determine whether you need the explanations or not. Keep introductions short if the children are ready to listen. Occasionally there is another activity going on in the room. Wait until they have opened their milk cartons for milk break and unwrapped their straws. Then ask, ''Are you ready?'' When they quiet down, begin.

First tell them, ''I am going to tell you a story called,'' giving them the name of the story. This sets a frame around the story and signals to them that this is the beginning. Now it is time to listen.

Look at your audience, smile, and begin. Watch the audience to be sure you are talking loudly and slowly enough. Try to keep the tempo lively, but clear. New storytellers often talk too fast, perhaps a sign of nervousness, and the children miss bits of the tale. Allow enough time for your listeners to react: to laugh, feel the tension, cry or squirm over the hero's plight. Children love to savor the happiness and sadness in their stories. Speaking too slowly can bore your listeners. If you listen to the story as you tell it and look at the flannelgraphs, you will naturally set your tempo at the right speed.

Slight differences in the voices of characters work well. Vary your voice in volume but this, too, comes naturally when you listen to yourself. The presentation will go well when you are aware that the children are not watching you perform. You are sharing a story with them.

Everything goes smoothly until . . . With young children there are always surprises. Something almost always goes wrong. The best way to meet the crisis is to remain calm.

When the felt board goes crashing to the ground, pick it up, smile and go on. Or joke about it. Say, ''Soon the earthquake was over,'' and go on with the story.

If the disturbance is just a cough or spilt milk, ignore it and go on with the story. If suddenly the children seem distracted, talk softer. They will quiet down to hear you. Or startle them with a loud expletive like ''Hey!'' or ''Well!'' accompanied by an emphatic gesture as if it were part of the story. Then proceed with the story.

Occasionally a child will interrupt with something he or she has to say. If it relates to the story and is a comment, smile and go on without commenting on the statement. If the child has a question about the story, answer it quickly and go on. If the statement is unrelated to the story, say, ''Let's talk about that after the story,'' and then go on.

Don't cut off the children's responses to the story, but if you spend time on questions and comments during the story, the thread of the narrative will be broken. Some children will forget what is going on in the story. Tell them you will talk about their interests after the story and be **sure** you do.

Once in a while something happens such as a fire drill that requires that the story stop. Although you may have gotten partly through the story, begin again from the beginning.

Watch the children as you recite the last paragraph. It's your reward. They smile, sigh, or stare off into space deep in thought. Sometimes the story weaves such a spell that they sit together in a moment of silence. When finished, allow a moment for reflection, then break the spell by saying, ''And that's the story called,'' and give the title again. This statement completes the frame built around the story. It signals that now they can ask questions.

Some groups will clap. They are clapping for the story and for your willingness to share it with them. Usually they all burst out talking simultaneously. Answer their questions, and talk a few minutes.

A disruptive child can cause problems. Muddle through the story for the sake of the other children, after stopping to ask the child to be quiet. After the story, give him the worst punishment possible—ask the child not to come to the next story time. Usually the disruptive child will decide it is a privilege to hear a story and return later and sit quietly.

Another problem is that children want to play with the flannel characters. Don't let them, especially if you plan to use them again, because they lose them or fight over the flannelgraphs. When you are finished, quickly put the characters in an envelope or folder to get them out of sight.

To meet the children's urge to manipulate the characters, a page of characters for the story "Soccer Spook" are provided in the activity section. With their own characters, they can play storyteller.

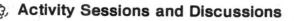

Activity Sessions and Discussions

After a brief period of comments and questions following a story, slip into a period of activities or discussions. Each story chapter includes several topics for discussion, suggestions for language development, games or activities. Occasionally there is a work sheet to duplicate for classroom use.

This activity session can be separated from the story by a period of time. It can be short or extended. It works both ways. The activities can be led by someone other than the storyteller. In team teaching, one person can learn the story to present to several classes, using the storyteller's time more efficiently. A second person can lead the discussions. Gear the length and extent of the activity to the age level, interests of the group, and time allowed. The activities can become almost as rewarding as telling the story, but nothing matches the magic of a shared story.

Story Hour

Each story chapter lists suggestions to incorporate each felt story into a story hour. Story hour is a misnomer because a story never lasts a full hour. Twenty minutes is long enough for preschoolers, and that time needs to be broken up with finger plays or some type of movement. There are many excellent books with finger plays and simple action songs that are loaded with suggestions for a stretch time. Two stories and a nursery rhyme or short poem are enough for preschoolers. Kindergartners will sit for a thirty-minute story hour of two stories and a narrative poem or if the stories are short, three. First graders can sit for thirty minutes. The stories can be more complicated than for kindergartners, but the children need a stretch or talk time in the middle. Second graders can last forty minutes with a break, but thirty-minute sessions without a wiggle break work better. Once second graders begin talking, it is often difficult to settle them down again even to listen to a story.

Build a story hour around a loose theme: pretend stories, legends, bear stories, city stories, seasonal stories. Don't plan a story hour around a moral theme. Children do not like to be lectured. A story or two with a moral is fine, but, for example, a story hour built around truthfulness using "Hopper's Whoppers" and other stories with a similar theme would annoy children. They expect a story hour to be fun. The only other purpose of a story hour is to introduce children to the rich variety of our language.

Enjoy story times. When those pudgy faces in front of you ease into smiles as your hero surmounts all difficulties at the end of the story, you will be glad you have shared the special magic bond of a good story with them.

Chapter II

No School—Not This Year

Josh could not wait![1] In two weeks he was going into the first grade. Already he had picked out what he wanted to wear the first day—his new blue shoes[2] and a green, spaceship shirt.[3] He even had a nifty schoolbag with **Josh** written on it.[4] Inside the bag were six long, sharpened pencils, a neat pad of paper, and three erasers. That day a letter came from school. Josh's mother read it to him.[5] It said,

Jackson Elementary School will begin the year on August 26. Josh Johnson will be in Mrs. Heatherfield's first grade class, room 8. He will ride bus 113 which will pick him up and drop him off at the corner of Lane and Elm.

"Oh no!" screamed Josh.[6] He ran to his room and hid under his favorite quilt. A few minutes later he felt safer. He put his new blue shoes in the back of his closet.[7] Then he hid his new shirt in a drawer under his winter pajamas,[8] and he stuffed the nifty schoolbag with **Josh** written across it under his bed.[9] He left the six pencils, pad of paper, and three erasers inside the schoolbag.

Then Josh went downstairs.[10] He announced to his mother, "I'm not going to school. No school—not this year."[11] Josh's mother didn't know what to do.

Ten[12] days before school started, his mother read Josh three nice books about school. "Well," she asked, "what do you think about school now?"

"No school," Josh said, "not this year."[13]

Nine[14] days before school started, Josh's father[15] drove Josh to Jackson Elementary School. Josh ran all over the playground. He climbed to the top of a jungle gym that looked like a giant bird's nest. He spun around on the swinging gate. Inside the brick building he found room 8, the gym, the library, and the lunch room. "Well," asked his father on the drive home, "What do you think about your school?"

"No school—not this year,"[16] Josh said.

Eight[17] days before school started, Josh's sister,[18] Sharon, told Josh about his teacher, Mrs. Heatherfield.[19] Sharon said that Mrs. H was nice. Her classes had fun, **and** last year they had gerbils in the room. Gerbils were Josh's favorite animal. "Well, what do you think about going to first grade now?" she asked.

Josh shook his head. "No school—not this year."[20]

It was **seven**[21] days before school started. Everyone in Josh's family[22] wanted to talk to Josh. Josh's mother[23] asked, "Why don't you want to go to school? School is a fun place."

"Yes, why?" asked his father.[24] "The building is pretty, and the playground is great."

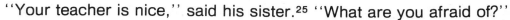

"Your teacher is nice," said his sister.[25] "What are you afraid of?"

Josh looked at the floor. Then he blurted out the truth. "The bus!"[26] he said. "Bus number 113. It's the bus that eats papers and jackets and mittens and books. Last year it gobbled up lots of your things!"

"It doesn't really eat those things," his sister said.

Josh looked straight at his sister. "Uh huh! Mommy said so," he said. "It ate your report card once. It might eat me."

Mother explained and explained that the bus just seemed to eat all the things that children forget and leave on the bus. "The things that seem to disappear turn up later in the lost and found," she said.

But Josh wasn't convinced. He crossed his arms stubbornly. He knew his mother was making up a story just to make him feel better.[27]

Six[28] days before school, Mother told Josh again that children leave their things on the bus.

Five[29] days until school, Mother told Josh that buses don't eat anything, except maybe gas and oil.

Four[30] days before school, Mother found Josh's new blue shoes[31] in the back of his closet and set them out for him to wear on the first day of school.

Three[32] days before school started, Josh's mother found his new shirt[33] under his winter pajamas and set it out next to his shoes.

Two[34] days before school, Josh's mother found his nifty schoolbag[35] with **Josh** written across it. She set it out next to his chair for Josh. Inside were his six, sharpened pencils, a neat pad of paper, and three clean erasers.

One[36] day before school started, Josh's mother said, "You are going to school."[37]

The next morning Josh put on his new blue shoes. He tucked his new, spaceship shirt into his jeans, and he carried his nifty schoolbag.[38] When the bus arrived,[39] Josh got on bus 113.[40]

All through the bumpy ride he clutched his schoolbag.[41] He looked around for clues to how the bus ate things.[42] He found none.[43]

A week went by. Josh relaxed his guard.

September 11th was a great day at school because Josh won a relay race in gym. Then it happened! Somewhere between school and home his nifty schoolbag with **Josh** written across it was lost[44]—**stolen**—EATEN! Josh was sure of it; **bus 113 had eaten his schoolbag.**[45]

Josh's father[46] drove him to school the next day. After reading group, Mrs. Heatherfield[47] told Josh that she had seen something of his in the lost and found box. On top of the half full, cardboard box lay his nifty schoolbag with **Josh** written across it.[48] Josh checked inside and found everything was just as he had left it. There were his six stubby, chewed pencils; a wrinkled, half-used pad of paper; and three dirty erasers.[49]

Josh's mother[50] was waiting for him at the bus stop after school. Josh bounded off the bus. "I found it," he announced. "The bus doesn't eat things."

"How do you know?" his mother asked.

Josh was astounded that his mother didn't know how he knew. So Josh told her. "Mrs. Heatherfield told me. **And she is always right**."[51]

From that day on Josh never thought that buses ate papers. Well, almost never. Once he had a messy writing paper with a frowny face on it. He folded the paper and put it in his pocket. When Josh's mother asked to see his papers for that day, he shoved the folded paper deeper into his pocket.[52] "Sorry," Josh said, "the bus ate it!"

Guideline for Telling the Story

Memorize the first and last paragraphs of "No School—Not This Year." In addition learn the sentence that ends at number 49, "There were his six stubby chewed pencils; a wrinkled, half-used pad of paper; and three dirty erasers." The humor of this sentence is lost if you forget to change the contents of Josh's bag.

Type the letter from school on a piece of white paper and read it, if you like. The advantage of having the letter to read is that you will be sure to say the date, room number, and bus number correctly. The disadvantage is that you have one more item to handle. Either way works fine.

Do not be surprised if the children join you when you say, "No school—not this year." They often also chime in during the countdown. If you would like them to join in, just mention it before you start the story.

Outline

I. Josh is excited about school.
   - A. He sets out his shoes, shirt and schoolbag.
   - B. His mother reads the letter from school.
   - C. Josh hides his shoes, shirt, and schoolbag.

II. Josh refuses to go to school.
   - A. His mother reads him books.
   - B. His father takes him to school.
   - C. His sister tells him about his teacher.

III. The whole family confronts Josh.
   - A. His mother asks why.
   - B. His father asks why.
   - C. His sister asks why.
   - D. Josh says he is afraid of the bus that eats things.
   - E. His mother tries to explain.

IV. The countdown to school begins.

V. Josh rides the bus to school.
   - A. He loses his schoolbag.
   - B. His father takes him to school.
   - C. He finds the schoolbag in the lost and found.
   - D. He tells his mother that the bus doesn't eat things.

Felt Characters and Props

1. Felt characters: Josh, Mother, Father, Sister, Mrs. Heatherfield, new **blue** shoes, **green** shirt, schoolbag, and bus number 113.
2. White piece of paper with the letter that Josh received from the school typed on it.
3. A piece of paper with the name of the story written on it. Fold this paper until it is very small and put it in your pocket. Be sure to wear something with a pocket.
4. Felt board and stand to hold up the board.
5. Text of the story, just in case.

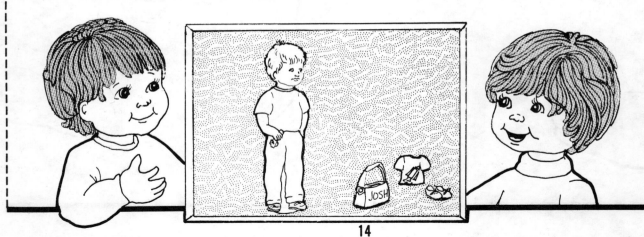

14

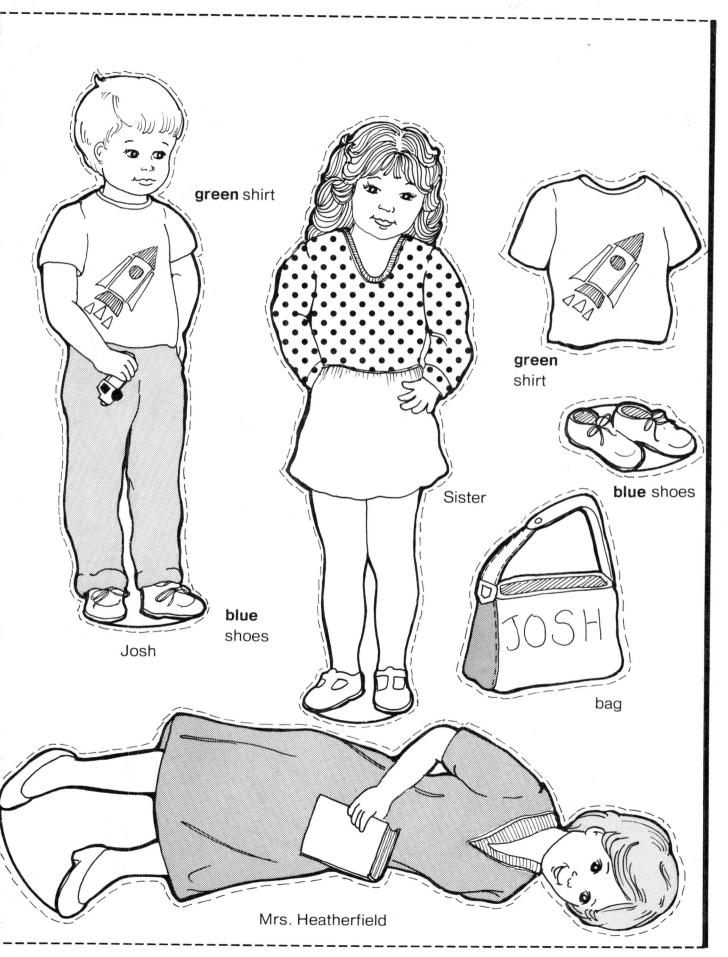

green shirt

green
shirt

blue shoes

Sister

JOSH

bag

blue
shoes

Josh

Mrs. Heatherfield

15

Father   Mother

16

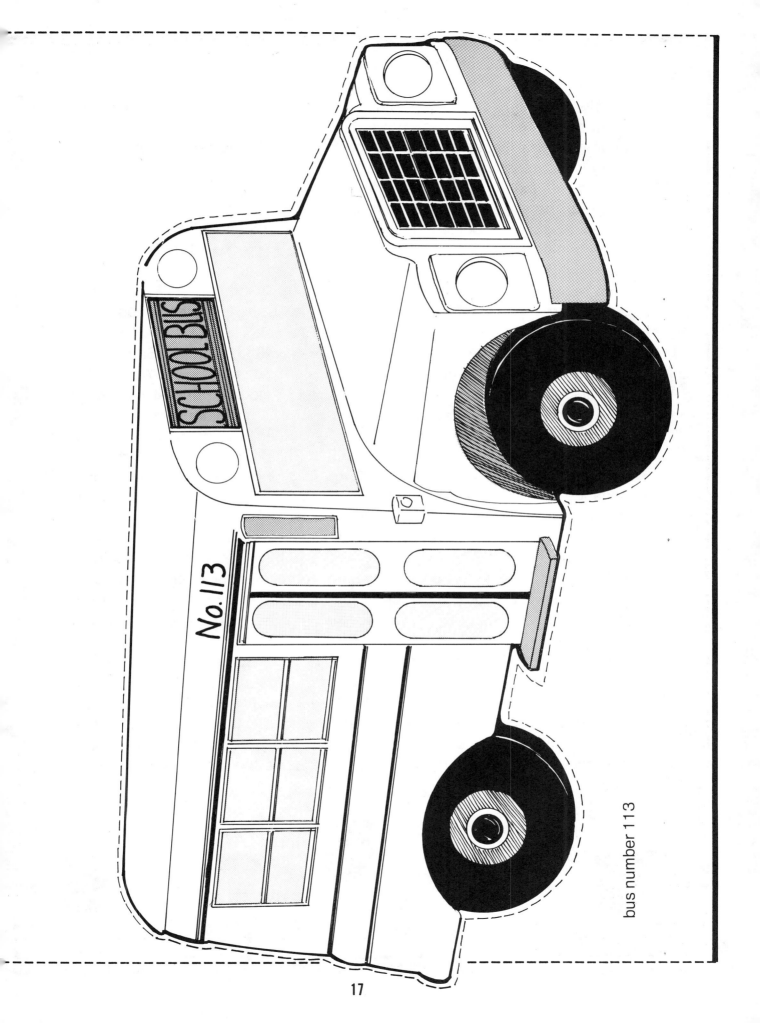

SCHOOL BUS

No. 113

bus number 113

Movements of the Felt Board Characters

"No School—Not This Year" has little physical action that requires movement of the felt characters. However, it is important to have the correct characters on the board. The flannelgraphs will help you remember the story's progression, often from Mother to Father to Sister.

Start with the felt board empty. At 1 push Josh in the middle of the board. At 2 put the shoes near a bottom corner. At 3 position the shirt near the shoes. Add the schoolbag at 4, placing it near the shoes and shirt. These three items will remain laid out in the corner of the board until Josh puts them away. At 5 add Mother. At 6 rush Josh off to one side. Remove Mother, then reposition Josh near the three articles near the corner. At 7 remove shoes from the board. At 8 remove the shirt. At 9 take off the schoolbag.

When part II begins, Josh is left alone on the board. At 10 put Mother next to Josh. Say the sentence before number 11 with emphasis. Shake your head and cross your arms stubbornly. At 12 hold up ten fingers. At 13 stubbornly shake your head and cross your arms. Remove Mother. At 14 hold up nine fingers. At 15 put Father next to Josh. At 16 shake your head and cross your arms. Take Father from the board, leaving Josh alone on the board. At 17 hold up eight fingers. At 18 position Sister next to Josh. At 19 bring out Mrs. Heatherfield (the teacher). Place her briefly on the board some distance from Josh and his sister. Then remove Mrs. Heatherfield. At 20 shake your head and cross your arms again.

As part III begins, Josh and his sister are on the board. At 21 hold up seven fingers. At 22 add Mother and Father. The four characters should be lined up across the board in this order: Mother, Father, Sister, and Josh. Keeping the characters in this order makes it easier to remember who talks next. At 23 add the bus. At 27 remove all the flannelgraphs except Josh and his Mother.

Part IV starts with Josh and his Mother on the board. At 28 hold up six fingers. Hold up five fingers at 29. At 30 hold up four fingers. At 31 put the shoes back on the board. At 32 hold up three fingers. At 35 place the schoolbag near the shirt and shoes. At 36 hold up one finger. The sentence before number 37 should be a command. Put your hands on your hips. Remove Mother, the shirt, and the shoes. Leave the schoolbag on the felt board.

Pause a few seconds before you begin section V. Josh is alone on the board with the schoolbag in one corner. At 38 pick up the schoolbag. Take the schoolbag and place it so that it looks like Josh is carrying it. Hold Josh and the schoolbag together with two fingers several inches in front of the flannel board. At 39 pick up the bus with your other hand. At 40 move Josh and the bag behind the bus. This is to give the illusion that he boarded the bus. The flannelgraphs of Josh and the schoolbag should be taken out of the audience's sight. Then the bus should be pressed against the felt. At 41 pretend you are clutching a schoolbag. Look scared. At 42 look all around. At 43 shrug. Remove the bus from the board. The felt board should now be empty. Place Josh in the center of the board.

At 50 put Mother in the center of the board. Hold Josh with his schoolbag in one hand. Hold the bus in front of him with the other hand. Move both hands (bus in front, Josh in back) onto the board. Slip Josh and the schoolbag from behind as you put the bus in the upper left-hand corner. It should look like Josh got off the bus with his schoolbag. Put Josh and his schoolbag next to Mother. Say the sentence before number 51 matter-of-factly. At 52 push your hand into your pocket.

Hints

Tell this story near the beginning of the school year. Be sure that younger children have gotten over their initial fear of riding the bus.

Wear a skirt or pants with a pocket. Have the folded piece of paper with the title on it stuffed in your pocket. Before beginning the story, pretend you forgot the name of the story. Reach down in your pocket and pull out the paper. Unfold it slowly and read the name of the story.

If you would like the children to join in at the countdown, ask them to. Participation seems to loosen up a small, quiet group. If your bunch is large or rowdy, don't ask them to chime in because they might spoil the story. Of course, they might join in regardless of your wishes.

Suggestions for Language Development, Discussion, and Creative Activities

Language Development: Explore the difference between what people say and what they mean. Josh heard a statement that buses seem to eat students' belongings. He thought that the bus actually did eat belongings in the same manner he eats food. He did not understand the figurative meaning that many items disappear as if the bus were eating them.

Talk about the statements that can be understood in more than one way. One type is the metaphor. **He is a tiger** meaning he is like a tiger. Another type includes homonyms. For example, **draw the drapes** can mean either to pull them closed or draw a picture of them. The Amelia Bedelia series by Peggy Parish has many examples of these dual meaning phrases. The terms **homonyms** and **metaphor** are beyond this age group. They will probably not be able to differentiate between the two groups, but they will be able to see that some statements can have two meanings. See how many examples they can think of.

Creative Writing: Have each person write or tell the steps he went through to get ready to go to school (or the library) that day. Be sure he tries to get the steps in logical order.

Art Activity: Find some pictures of early schools in your area. Explain briefly how they were different from schools today. Then give everyone paper and an art media (markers, crayons, colored pencils, or paints). Ask them to draw pictures of what a school room might look like in one hundred years.

Songs: The two songs ''Mary Had a Little Lamb'' and ''The Wheels of the Bus Go Round and Round,'' listed in the Resources section, would fit between the story and one of the desk activities.

Resources for a Story Hour

School Days

Books:

Crow Boy by Taro Yashima. Viking, 1955. (A sensitive story of a Japanese schoolboy.)

Glenda by Janice Udry. Harper, 1969. (A witch brews mischief at school.)

Miss Nelson Is Missing by Harry Allard. Houghton Mifflin, 1982. (Miss Nelson is replaced by Viola Swamp when the children misbehave.)

The New Teacher by Miriam Cohen. Macmillan, 1972. (Simple. The new teacher is not frightening as the children had imagined.)

No School Today by Franz Brandenberg. Scholastic, 1975.

Poems:

''First Day of School.'' From *I Wonder How, I Wonder Why* by Aileen Fisher. Abelard-Schuman, 1962. (unpaged)

''Miss Norma Jean Pugh, First Grade Teacher'' by Mary O'Neill. From *Time for Poetry* compiled by M. H. Arbuthnot and S. L. Root, Jr. Scott, Foresman, 1967, p. 8.

''School Is Over'' by Kate Greenaway. From *Time for Poetry* compiled by M. H. Arbuthnot and S. L. Root, Jr. Scott, Foresman, 1967, p. 84.

Songs:

''Mary Had a Little Lamb.'' From *The New Golden Song Book*. Golden Press, 1965.

''The Wheels of the Bus Go Round and Round.'' From *The Wheels of the Bus Go Round and Round* collected by Nancy Larrick. Golden Gate, 1972, p. 6. (Popular bus song with motions.)

Chapter III

Mysterious Number Six*

It is Halloween night.[1] Someone is in a dancer's pink dress. She sits alone under a big tree. It is getting dark. The moon is bright. The wind blows. The leaves move.

CRUNCH! Who is coming? A little devil.[2] A big white ghost.[3] A huge pumpkin.[4] A funny clown.[5] A little witch.[6]

"Are we all here?" the dancer asks.

"Let's count and see," says the ghost.

They count. "One, dancer;[7] two, devil;[8] three, ghost;[9] four, pumpkin;[10] five, clown;[11] six, witch."[12]

"Six?"

"Only five animals were to meet here. Only five. Not six. Our Halloween party was for five," says the dancer.

"Who else is here?" asks the devil.

"Whooo," the owl in the tree says. They jump.

Pig, Duck, Cow, Horse, and Dog are in their Halloween costumes. So is someone else. Who is the dancer? Who is the pumpkin? Who is the ghost? Who is the clown? Who is the witch? Who is the devil? Who is Mysterious Number Six?

"Let's guess and see who is here," oinks the dancer. "Guess who I am."[13] She turns around and around.

The sheet with the pumpkin head guesses. "You are fat. You spin nicely. You like pink. Did you oink?"

"Yes," she says.

"You are Pig."

Right![14] Now I will guess," Pig says. "Ghost is tall.[15] He is also long. He is the biggest one here. Ghost, are you Cow?"

"Neigh,"[16] says the ghost.

"Oh, Horse," Pig says.[17] She giggles and spins.

Ghost slips off the sheet. "Now, I can see better."

"Who am I?" the clown asks.[18] His big ears slip out from under his hat. The dot in the tail of the clown wags.

Horse wiggles his ears. "You are Dog. Am I right?"

"Yes," Dog says.[19] His tail wags and wags and wags. "My turn to guess."

*First published in *Children's Playmate Magazine*, 1978, Indianapolis, Indiana.

He walks around the little red devil, the big pumpkin head, and the little witch. "Pumpkin has four big brown feet.[20] I see them. You are as big as Horse. Are you Cow?"

"Yes," Cow moos softly.[21] "I will guess the devil."[22]

"Quack," the devil says.

"I see yellow feet. You have a long beak. You did quack. Duck, is that you?" Cow asks.

"Quack yes," says Duck.[23] "That is all five of us."

The five look at the witch. "Who are you? Take off the mask."

The witch looks down.[24] No one talks. "I don't have a mask on," she says.

"What? No mask. She's a real witch!" Pig shouts.

"I'm Spook, a real Halloween witch. I wanted to play, too. I wanted to go to a real Halloween party. I don't like flying around and scaring people."

The animals looked at one another. "I'm scared," one says.

"Sh, she will hear," Duck says. "Let her stay."

They agree. Spook sees a real Halloween party. The animals see a real witch. They even ride on her broom. They all have a really happy Halloween.

Look in the sky on Halloween night. Is there a horse, pig, cow, dog, or duck riding behind a little witch? It might be Spook and her new friends.

Guideline for Telling the Story

This story is the easiest story to tell in the book because the movements consist only of placing the characters on the board and unmasking them. The text is both short and logical. Three short paragraphs should be memorized: the first, last, and Spook's speech after number 24 that begins "I'm Spook, a real Halloween witch."

Outline

I. A dancer waits on Halloween night.
    A. The characters arrive in costume.
    B. They count to see if everyone is there.
    C. Who is Pig, Duck, Cow, Horse, and Dog?
    D. Who is Mysterious Number Six?
II. They guess who is under the costumes.
    A. Pumpkin guesses the dancer (Pig).
    B. Pig guesses the ghost (Horse).
    C. Horse guesses the clown (Dog).
    D. Dog guesses the pumpkin (Cow).
    E. Cow guesses the devil (Duck).
III. The witch is Spook, a real witch.
    A. The animals let her stay.
    B. They have a good Halloween party.

Felt Characters and Props

1. Felt characters: **pink** Pig dressed as a dancer, Duck dressed as a devil, Horse dressed as a ghost, Cow dressed as a pumpkin, Dog dressed as a clown, and Spook the witch. These characters that unmask are worth the small added effort. First, cut out the costumed characters and color them. Secondly, cut out the faces that go behind the costumes. Color them. Position the animals behind the costumes so the shapes match and glue the tabs of the animals to the backs of the costumes. Add the felt last. After the characters are dry, fold the masks down to reveal the animals beneath. The masks can be kept up with small plastic paper clips if they fall.
2. Felt board and stand.
3. Text of the story.

pink Pig dressed as dancer
(Top section)

fold line

Spook the witch

tab

pink pig face that goes under dancer

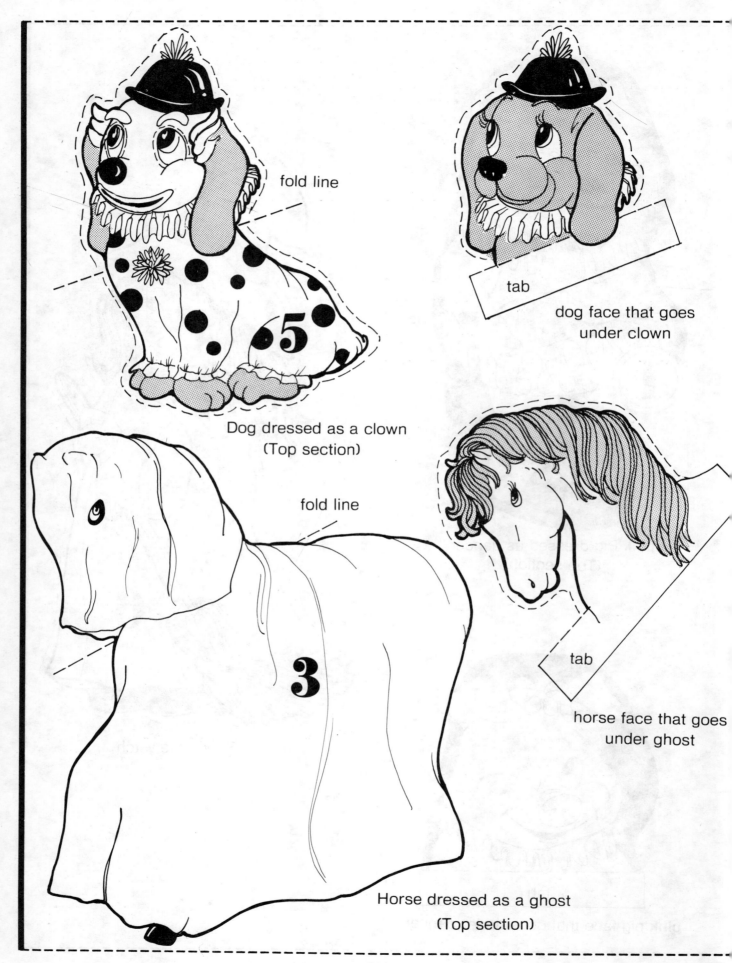

fold line

dog face that goes
under clown

tab

Dog dressed as a clown
(Top section)

fold line

3

tab

horse face that goes
under ghost

Horse dressed as a ghost
(Top section)

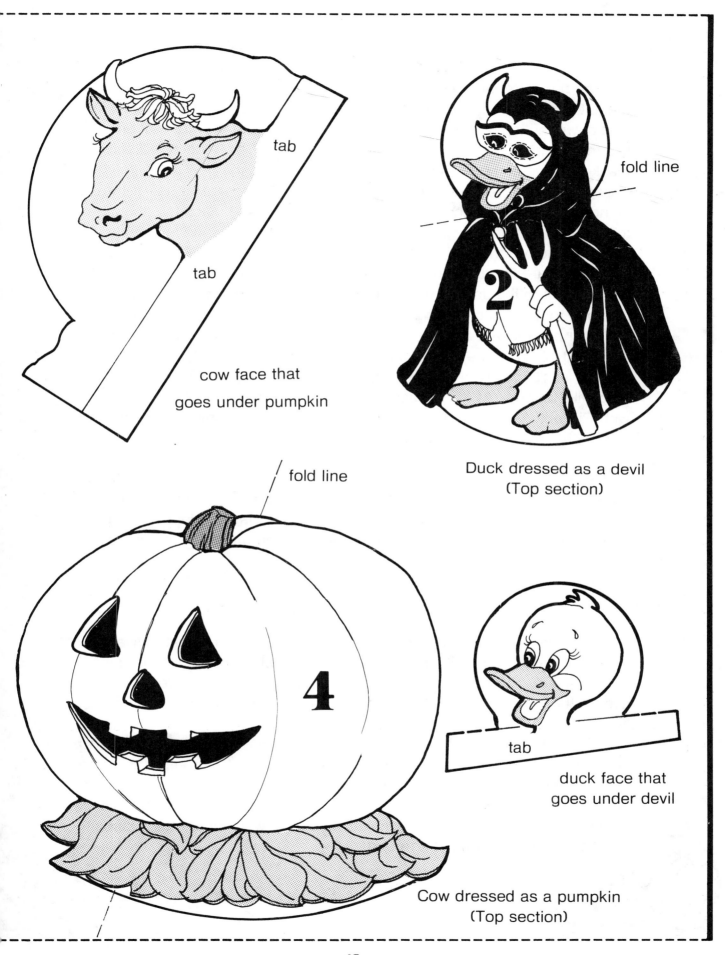

tab

tab

cow face that
goes under pumpkin

fold line

2

Duck dressed as a devil
(Top section)

fold line

4

tab

duck face that
goes under devil

Cow dressed as a pumpkin
(Top section)

Movements of the Felt Board Characters

Once the six characters for ''Mysterious Number Six'' are arranged on the felt board, they are moved only a little. As each character is unmasked, turn down the top of the figure along the fold line. With the larger characters like the pumpkin and ghost, a paper clip at the top when the characters are masked prevents accidental flopping down of the paper.

Begin with the felt board empty. At 1 add the dancer. Put her at the audience's left. At 2 put the devil next to the dancer. At 3 place the ghost next to the devil. At 4 add the pumpkin. At 5 put the clown next to the pumpkin. At 6 place the witch at the audience's right side of the board. The six characters are lined up numbering one through six from the left to right.

At 7 point to the dancer. At 8 point to the devil. At 9 point to the ghost. At 10 point to the pumpkin. At 11 point to the clown. At 12 point to the witch.

Part II begins with all six characters remaining in their lineup across the board. At 13 move the dancer slightly down on the board. At 14 unmask the dancer. At 15 move the ghost down on the board level with the dancer. At 16 neigh like a horse. At 17 unmask the ghost. At 18 move the clown down level with Pig and Horse. At 19 unmask the clown. At 20 move pumpkin down level with the others. At 21 unmask the pumpkin. At 22 move the devil down. Unmask the devil at 23.

Part III begins with the six characters in a line as they were in part II. The witch is higher than the other characters. At 24 take the witch from the right side of the board and move her to the left. She is now facing the other characters. The characters remain in this position until the story ends.

Hints

''Mysterious Number Six'' is a Halloween story and is most effective when told near Halloween. Tell it in a darkened room with light focused on the felt board. A jack-o'-lantern sitting nearby adds a holiday touch. Be sure not to overdo the spooky atmosphere because some kindergartners frighten easily.

Precede the story with a brief mention of our custom of dressing up on Halloween. ''Have you ever dressed up on Halloween?'' prompts stories of what the children were or want to be for Halloween. Explain that another custom is that everyone tries to guess who is under each custume. This explanation will enlighten anyone who is not familiar with our custom, especially those from a foreign background.

Suggestions for Language Development, Discussion, and Creative Activities

Language Development: Discuss the sounds in the story—the leaves crunching, the owl hooting, the animals oinking, neighing, and quacking. Discuss the sights in the story—the costumes, the tree. What other ways could you learn about something? Taste, smell, and feel. Have the children give examples of ways that their five senses learn about things. (For example: I feel the heat from the sun on my face. I tasted the sweet chocolate candy.)

Creative Writing: "Mysterious Number Six" is set under a tree on Halloween night. Discuss other places that would be a good place for a Halloween story (for example: a haunted house, ghost town, door-to-door in the neighborhood). What things might you see, hear, feel, smell, or taste in these places? Have each student write a short paragraph describing a place that would be good for a Halloween story by using sensory words.

Feel Guessing Game: The animals in the story guessed who was under each costume because they had clues. Size, shape, the noise the animal made were clues. Take several objects that the children are familiar with. Hide each object in a numbered paper bag. One at a time each child puts a hand in each bag. Then each child guesses on paper what is in each bag from the clues of size, shape, and feel.

Smell Guessing Game: Put solid objects with strong smells in clean socks and tie the ends (for example: onion, orange, garlic, peppermint, dirt, scented candles, candy). Let the children guess what is in the socks.

Resources for a Story Hour

Halloween

Books:

A Dark, Dark Tale by Ruth Brown. Dial, 1981. (Colorful and simple.)

The Gobble-uns'll Git You if You Don't Watch Out! by James Whitcomb Riley. Lippincott, 1975. (Black and white illustrations and a popular poem.)

Tiger Called Thomas by Charlotte Zolotow. Lothrop, 1966. (A favorite gentle picture book.)

Woggle of Witches by Adrienne Adams. Scribner, 1971. (Short, simple, and full color.)

Poems:

''The Goblin'' by Rose Fyleman. From *Time for Poetry* compiled by May Hill Arbuthnot. Scott, Foresman, 1952, p. 132.

''My Brother'' by Dorothy Aldis. From *Time for Poetry* compiled by May Hill Arbuthnot. Scott, Foresman, 1952, p. 163.

''The Quiet Child'' by Rachel Field. From *Songs the Sandman Sings* compiled by Gwendolyn Reed. Atheneum, 1969, p. 39.

Songs:

''Skin and Bones.'' From *Hi! Ho! The Rattlin' Bog* selected by John Langstaff. Harcourt, Brace & World, 1969. (Music and words of the Kentucky ghost song. A favorite of singing storytellers.)

Records:

Halloween Songs That Tickle Your Funny Bone by Ruth Roberts. Michael Brent Publishers, 1974. (Familiar songs made into fun Halloween songs. A booklet gives words and music, too.)

Filmstrips:

The Ghost with the Halloween Hiccups by Stephen Mooser. Educational Enrichment Materials, 1979. (39 frames.)

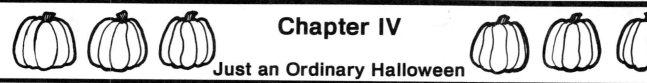
It was the Halloween of '86, just an ordinary Halloween with parties, costumes, and jack-o'-lanterns. And as is customary on ordinary Halloweens, there was a girl waiting for her guests to arrive for her Halloween party.[1] Becky was her name. And she was dressed like the biggest carrot you would ever see. She had invited everyone in her class at school to the party, even the kids she didn't know very well. She had planned an ordinary party of games, treats, and costume contests. Becky's mother, dressed as the storytelling ghost, was going to tell spooky tales.

Some folks like the scaring best on Halloween. Some are fond of the candy. Some can't wait to play pranks. Some like to pretend they are someone else. Now Becky, she liked making up costumes best. She'd made her carrot costume from an old, orange curtain and some green crepe paper. The thing she wasn't good at was the pretending. She always gave herself away by giggling and saying she was Becky. Becky wished she could pretend so well that no one could guess who she was.

Now standing in front of your house fifteen minutes before your party begins doesn't often produce an early guest, but Becky was in luck. Down the street came a girl in blue jeans and a silver shirt.[2] Becky figured that she was the blonde head that sat three rows in front of her. She couldn't remember her name. Her costume wasn't very good. Becky couldn't even figure out what she was supposed to be. She had a funny-looking calculator strapped on her belt. She wore a silver shirt with a super silver necklace. Other than that she looked perfectly ordinary.

Becky asked her, "What are you?"

The girl, looked straight into the carrot's eyes and said, "I'm Lison from the planet Zix. I've come down to earth to visit you."[3]

Right then, Becky knew she liked this Lison. Here was a girl who wasn't good at costumes, but she was terrific at pretending. And **Lison**, that was a great space name. Lison wouldn't give herself away by giggling, like Becky always did. Becky whispered to Lison,[4] "I'm glad you've come to my party. Don't tell your real name. We'll guess later."

And that Lison, she went right on pretending.[5] "Party? Do you earthlings have parties, too?" she asked.

Becky giggled and whispered, "I'm Becky." Oops.[6] There she went giving herself away again. As I said, Becky was good at costumes, but not at pretending.[7]

Now Becky hated to see Lison's good performance wasted. Everyone would guess her without a better costume. So Becky offered to help Lison fix up her costume. With the dress-up stuff Becky had in the basement, it would be easy.

Becky scrounged through a trunk of dress-up clothes. The first thing she found was a pair of boots.[8] She helped Lison into her father's old galoshes. To make them even spacier, Becky added wires, dials, and reflectors from Dad's parts box.

No space creature should be without antennae.[9] So Becky fashioned a pair with four paper cups and some aluminum foil.

Lison was beginning to look a little alien, but not weird enough to suit Becky. Next she added oversized gloves.[10] She tucked one finger of the gloves inside so Lison looked like she had only three fingers and one thumb.

Lison was enjoying the dressing up almost as much as Becky was. They added a hat, some green makeup to Lison's face, and huge goggles.[11] Becky gave Lison her Space Alien laser gun.[12] She'd gotten that toy last Christmas. Lison looked exactly like a space creature from the planet Zix should look.

After all this pretending and dressing up, Becky almost forgot about the other guests and the party. Of course, when the doorbell rang[13] and there stood a ghost,[14] a clown,[15] two Darth Vaders,[16] a ballerina,[17] and a bat,[18] she remembered.

One of the best ordinary Halloween parties got underway. They ate spooky sandwiches and drank witches brew. The big, black pot was full of candy and wrapped surprises. They played games and, of course, everyone tried to guess who was who. The first person guessed was—[19] that's right—Becky. She giggled and everyone knew. And would you believe it,[20] Lison was the only one no one could guess. She won the big prize, the huge jack-o'-lantern with the flashlight in it.[21]

Instead of revealing her identity, like Becky would have done, Lison, gave a big smile and said, "Thank you. I invite you all to come with me sometime to visit my planet, Zix. I brought my small spaceship today. It holds only me, but next time, I'll bring the big one so you all can come back with me."

Everyone loved her pretending. "Where is Zix?" a Darth Vader asked.[22]

Lison pointed out the window at a bright star. "It's right past the Milky Way. We're the third planet from our sun, just like you are."

A big, white sheet fluttered into the room moaning, "Whooo."[23] She dimmed the lights so only Lison's pumpkin was lighted. "I'm the ghostly storyteller," Becky's mother said from under the sheet. She told tales so spooky that everyone's neck prickled.

Before you could say "boo," the party was over and all the guests were gone,[24] except Lison. Even after she took off the costume Becky had loaned her,[25] she was still pretending. She invited Becky to walk her to her spaceship.

Becky straightened up and tried to act like a carrot—crunchy or nutritious or vegetable-like. "This carrot will walk the space creature home—I mean to your spaceship." So Becky giggled all the way down the street with her new friend.

When they came to an overgrown lot, Lison started into the lot. Becky hung back remembering the spooky tales of ghosts and witches.

"Come on," Lison said.

Becky stepped cautiously into dark masses of greenery. Behind the bushes shimmered a silver spaceship.[26] Before Becky could open her mouth and gasp, Lison stepped into it. She put her necklace into Becky's hand and said, "See you," just like an ordinary kid. But Lison wasn't an ordinary kid! She **was** from another planet.[27] Lison's ship took off with a whoosh and a twinkle of lights. Becky blinked as the silver ball headed straight for a star on the other side of the Milky Way.

Becky looked at the silver necklace that Lison had given her. Lison's voice came from the necklace. "Thanks, Becky. I can't wait to have my own Halloween party on Zix. I'll show everyone how to dress up like space creatures." The lights on the spaceship blinked twice, and Lison was gone.

Of all the Halloweens that have come and gone, Becky will never forget the Halloween of '86, the ordinary party and her extraordinary guest.

Guideline for Telling the Story

Tell this tale in a folksy tone. Put a twinkle in your eye. Change the year in the first and last sentences to the current year. No memorization is necessary for this story. The only parts that might be learned verbatim are the second paragraph, "Some folks like the scaring . . ." and the third paragraph from the end, "Becky stepped cautiously into dark masses of greenery."

Differentiate the speech of Lison (formal), Becky (giggly), and the narrator (folksy).

Elongate the moaning sound of the "Whoo" at number 23.

Outline

I. Becky waits for her guests to come to her Halloween party.
       A. She likes making up costumes.
       B. She isn't good at pretending.

II. A guest comes down the street.
       A. Lison says she is from the planet Zix.
       B. She pretends well, but her costume isn't good.

III. Becky offers to fix up Lison's costume.
       A. She adds boots.
       B. She makes antennae from paper cups and foil.
       C. She adds oversized gloves.
       D. She adds a hat, green makeup, and goggles.
       E. Lastly, she adds a toy space gun.

IV. The rest of the guests arrive.
       A. No one can guess who Lison is.
       B. Lison continues pretending she is from outer space.
       C. The ghostly storyteller tells her stories.
       D. The party is over.

V. Lison takes off her costume but still pretends.
       A. She asks Becky to walk her "home."
       B. They cross an overgrown lot.
       C. Becky sees the spaceship.
       D. Lison gives Becky a necklace.
       E. The spaceship takes off.
       F. The necklace talks.

Felt Characters and Props

1. Felt characters: Becky dressed as a carrot (**orange** suit with **green** headdress), storytelling ghost, group of costumed friends, jack-o'-lantern, spaceship, Lison (**blond** hair, **blue** jeans, **silver** shirt, **silver** necklace), and the parts to the costume added to Lison: pair of boots, two antennae, two gloves, face covering (hat, goggles and **green** makeup), and a laser gun. For four parts of the costume (the two gloves, the face covering, and the pair of boots), the felt that surrounds them needs to be bigger to hold them on the board. The solid lines indicate where these parts need to be cut out. The dotted line indicates the shape of the felt that goes behind the parts and shows where the parts should be glued to the felt. There is a separate pattern for the felt for these four costume parts.
2. A felt board covered in black and a stand to hold up the board.
3. Text of the story, just in case.

group of costumed friends

green headdress

orange suit

Becky

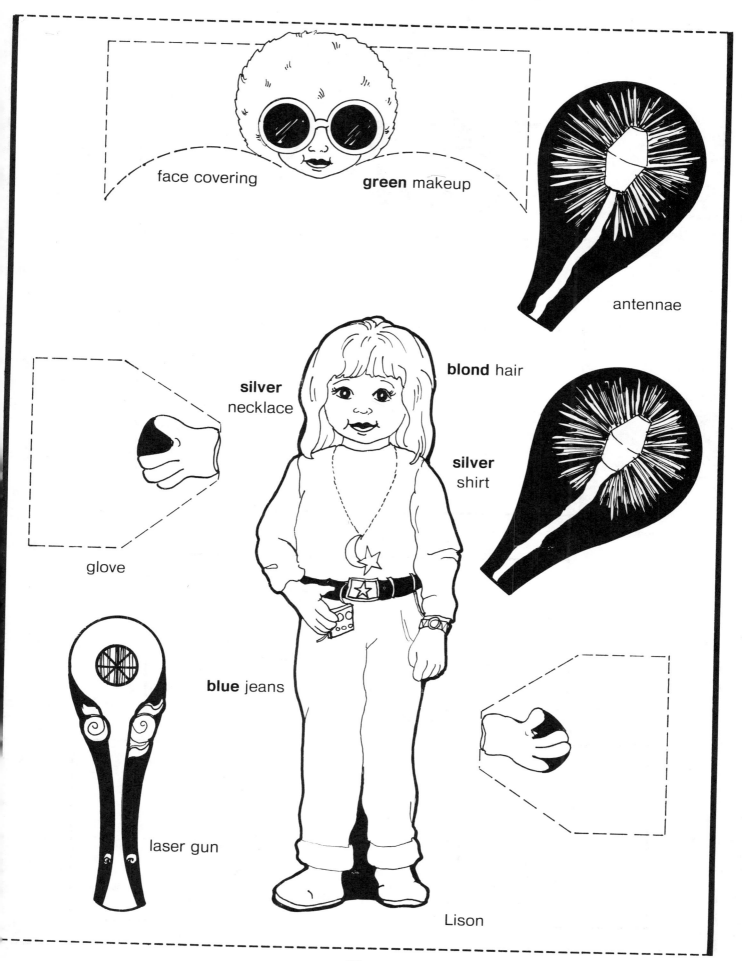

face covering

green makeup

antennae

silver necklace

blond hair

silver shirt

glove

blue jeans

laser gun

Lison

37

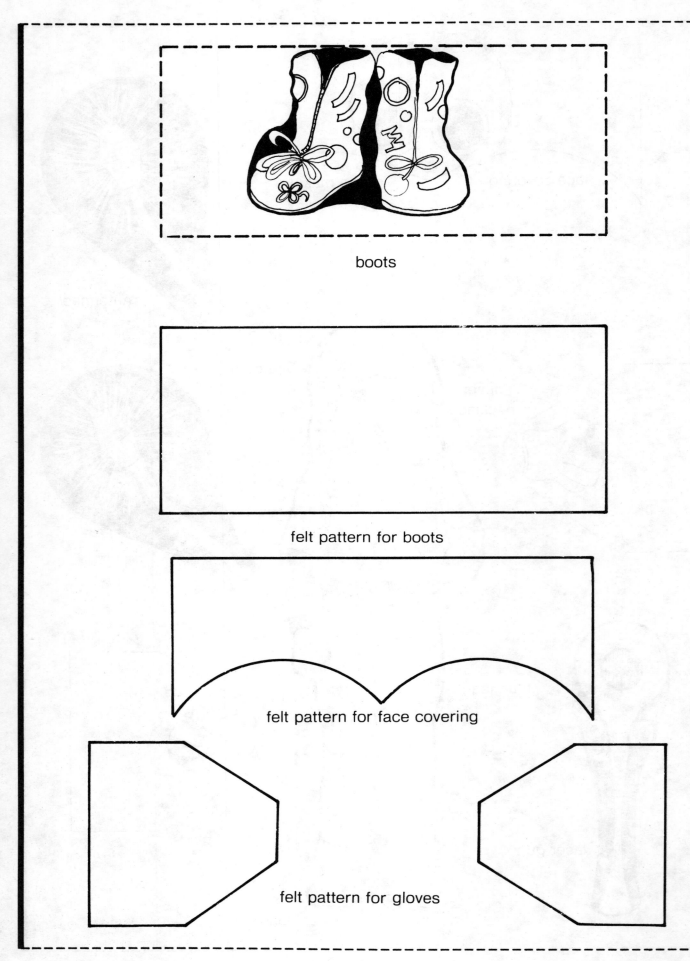

boots

felt pattern for boots

felt pattern for face covering

felt pattern for gloves

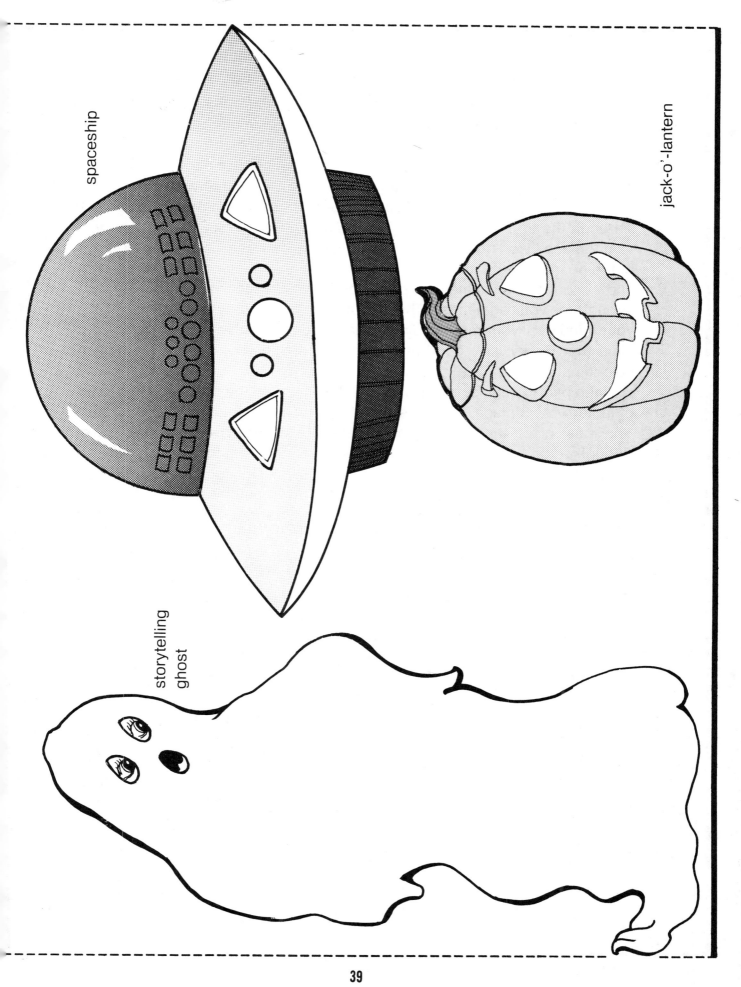

spaceship

jack-o'-lantern

storytelling ghost

Movements of the Felt Board Characters

"Just an Ordinary Halloween" has more flannelgraphs than most of the other stories, but the movements are not more difficult. Seven of the flannelgraphs are pieces of a costume that fit over the Lison character. Once you have practiced the story, the movements will be simple to remember.

Begin with a blank flannel board. Place the jack-o'-lantern in a lower corner before you begin the story. At 1 place Becky in the center of the board. Through the first two paragraphs of the story, Becky remains stationary.

At 2 place Lison on the board about halfway between Becky and the edge of the board. When Lison describes who she is at 3, stand or sit up straight and announce her name and planet proudly. Whisper at 4 in a voice loud enough for your audience to hear. Put your hands on your hips at 5. Clap your hand over your mouth as if you had made a mistake at 6. While you explain that Becky isn't good at pretending, shake your head. This motion belongs at number 7.

When part III begins, only Becky and Lison are on the board with the jack-o'-lantern. At 8 place the boots over the shoes of the Lison felt character. You must place the costume parts carefully so they overhang the figure. Enough of the felt on the back of the costume must meet the flannel board so the costume will stick. Add the antennae at 9, pausing long enough to position them. At 10 add the gloves one at a time. At 11 add the goggles, hat, and makeup. Lastly, at 12 add the laser gun. Do not try to move Lison until her costume is removed. Move other characters around her.

At 13 add the other guests. The guests are one flannelgraph. Point to the ghost at 14, the clown at 15, the Darth Vaders at 16, the ballerina at 17, and the bat at 18. Pause at 19 to give your audience a chance to respond. Some audiences will chime in with "Becky." Others will say nothing. If they say nothing, just go on. Pause at 20 and emphasize "Lison was the only one no one could guess." At 21 move the pumpkin next to Lison. Point to a Darth Vader at 22. At 23 moan "Whoo." Repeat "whoo" as many times as you like. Then place the ghost on the board. Be sure not to disturb the Lison character with all her costume parts. At 24 remove the ghost and the guests.

Lison in her costume, Becky, and the jack-o'-lantern remain on the board when the last section of the story begins. At number 25 remove the boots, gloves, antennae, mask, and gun from the Lison character. The Lison flannelgraph should now be without a costume. At 26 pop the spaceship onto the board next to Becky. At 27 pick up the Lison flannelgraph, put the spaceship in front of her, and remove them. The story ends with only Becky on the board.

Hints

This story takes place around Halloween. It could be used in October, but it could also be told at another time. Whenever you tell it, keep the tone folksy and relaxed.

Your listeners need to know what **ordinary** means to grasp the humor of the tale. Before the story, explain the meaning of the word **ordinary**. Say, "**Ordinary** means not special or unusual. On an **ordinary** day, nothing different happens, only the usual things. Nothing exciting happens. An **ordinary** day is not necessarily bad. It's just a regular day."

Then explain what **extraordinary** means. "**Extraordinary** means special or unusual. On an **extraordinary** day something special or unusual happens."

Lastly, tell them that this is the story about an **ordinary** Halloween party, just a regular, plain old Halloween party.

Suggestions for Language Development, Discussion, and Creative Activities

Language Development: This story is a fantasy. Fantasies are made by asking **what if** something happened. Brainstorm in a group and make up some **what if's** about Halloween. For example, **what if** you went to 60 houses and got tons of candy. What might happen? **What if** you turned into what you are dressed up to be. **What if** you lost your little sister trick or treating? **What if** you met a real witch?

What If Game: This is a variation of the round robin story designed to help children to learn to plot stories by asking the question "what if?" Begin a story, "Once upon a time in a faraway land a little girl and her brother were strolling in the forest." Hand the storytelling wand (a ruler or pencil will do) to the next person. This person asks a "what if" question. For example, he or she might ask, "What if they fell into a hole?" Then that child passes on the wand to the next child in the circle. The child tries to make up a solution. For example, "The girl climbs on the boy's shoulders and gets out and then throws him a rope." The wand is passed. The next child asks a "what if" question, and so on, in the same manner.

Art Activity: Becky liked to plan costumes. On the following activity page are drawings of three children. Give your students fabric scraps, yarn, markers, crayons, and paints so they can design **extraordinary** costumes for the three figures. Be sure to tell your group that the clothes that the figures have on are **not** part of the costume. The clothes that are shown are worn under the costume for warmth. Halloween nights are usually chilly. Challenge them to think up a name for each costume after they have finished. Offer prizes for the prettiest, scariest, weirdest, most original, and funniest designs.

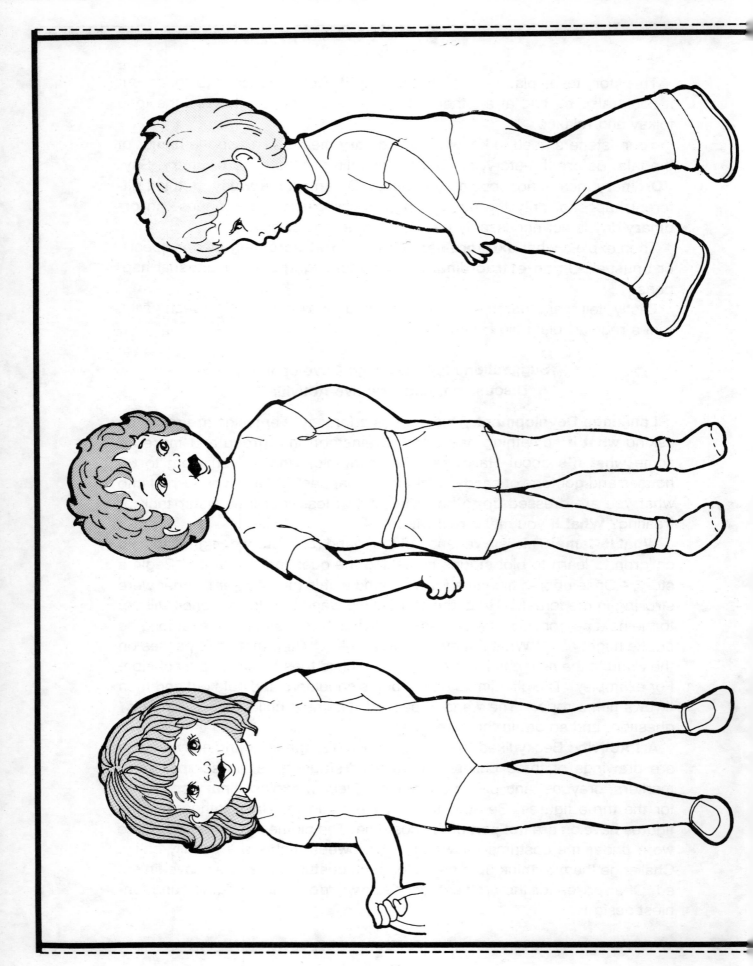

Resources for a Story Hour

Parties

Books:

The Animal Kids by Lorinda Bryan Cauley. G. P. Putnam's Sons, 1979. (Sly humor and simple text about a party just for animals makes this book a hit.)

Fortunately by Remy Charlip. Four Winds, 1964. (Simple, fun, and colorful. Fortunate and unfortunate things happen to Ned on his way to a surprise party.)

Paul's Christmas Birthday by Carol Carrick. Greenwillow, 1978. (A birthday near Christmas turns out fine.)

Python's Party by Brian Wildsmith. Watts, 1974. (Beautiful, colorful illustrations.)

The Queen and Rosie Randall by Helen Oxenbury. Morrow, 1979. (A humorous story about a tea party for the king.)

Songs:

"The Unbirthday Song" by Mack David, Al Hoffman, and Jerry Livingston. From *The Walt Disney Song Book*. Golden Press, 1979. (A favorite song from the Disney version of *Alice in Wonderland*.)

Poems:

"A Party." From *Tirra Lirra* by Laura E. Richards. Little Brown, 1955, p. 100.

"The Saturday's Party in Fairyland" by M. C. Davis. From *A Treasury of Verse for Little Children*, selected by M. G. Edgar. Crowell, 1936, p. 140.

Filmstrips:

The Stupids Have a Ball by Harry Allard. Educational Enrichment Materials, 1980. (40—60 frames.)

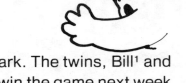

Chapter V

Soccer Spook

Soccer practice was over because it was getting dark. The twins, Bill[1] and Will[2] were walking home. Will said,[3] "We're going to win the game next week against the girls because we always get the good practice field."

"It doesn't seem fair," Bill said.[4] "Alice never gets home from trumpet lessons on time. She's always late, so the girls don't ever get the good field."[5]

"That's their problem," said Will.

The twins had a long walk home. On the side of the street where the boys were walking, there was on old, empty house. The kids at school called it the haunted house. The twins did not really believe in haunted houses,[6] but the bigger boys told them stories about that house. Strange stories![7]

Bill and Will were near the crooked gate to the house when they heard it. "Whoo.[8] Whoo. I'm gonna get you! Whoo. Whoo. I'm gonna get you!" They stood like statues, but their eyes looked around.[9] Something white and fluttery sprung out of the bushes.[10] Bill and Will turned around and sped back down Periwinkle Lane.[11]

They stopped at Tim and Imogene Taylor's house. Tim[12] was captain of the boys' soccer team. His sister was captain of the girls' team.[13] The twins told Tim about the ghost. Imogene overheard.

"Scaredy-cats," Imogene said.[14] "Wait until I tell the girls."

Bill begged, "Please don't."

"Someone is trying to scare you," Tim said.

"Someone **is** scaring me!" said Will.

"Let's stop practicing soccer until dark," said Bill.

"No!" Tim said. "That's not the answer."

Mr. Taylor drove the twins home.[15] He, too, told them there were no such things as ghosts.[16]

The next evening the twins didn't want to go to practice. They dillydallied too long and were late. So the girls' team practiced on the big field. The first team with all players at the park got the good field. That was the rule.

Practice ended early.[17] Armed with a flashlight, Tim and Imogene followed the twins down Periwinkle Lane.[18] Bill and Will were beside the gate to the haunted house when something howled, "Whoo. Whoo. I'm gonna get you." A white shape jumped out at the twins.[19]

"Ahhh," screamed Bill.[20] He could not decide whether to hide his eyes or run away. He did both. He tripped and fell, and Will fell on top of Bill.[21]

Imogene and Tim hurdled the pile of twins[22] and chased the ghost down the street[23] and around the house.[24] Then they followed the ghost back up the street.[25] Plink. Plonk. Plinkity, plonk.[26] The ghost was dropping little things on the sidewalk. Plink. Plonk. Plinkity, plonk.[27] Tim aimed his flashlight at the round things. They were jelly beans. Ghosts don't eat jelly beans; kids do.

Tim's flashlight shone on a white sheet. Under the sheet were tennis shoes with untied, orange laces.

The ghost ran back toward the haunted house. Tim and Imogene followed. The twins still sat by the gate rubbing their sore knees. "Ohhhh. Here it comes!" Tim yelled, "Bill! Will! Stop that ghost!"

Bill looked at the ghost. Will looked at the ghost. Then Bill looked at Will. The twins backed away from the ghost.[29]

Imogene had an idea. "Scaredy-cats! You're scaredy-cats!" she shouted.

"Are not!" yelled Will. Bill and Will faced the ghost with their arms outstretched.[30] Bill closed his eyes,[31] but it was too dark for the ghost to tell.

When the ghost slowed down in front of the twins, Tim and Imogene tackled the ghost.[32] They pulled off the sheet.[33] It was Alice.

"Why?" Imogene asked.

"To make them miss practice," Alice said. "That way we girls would have a chance at the big game."

"Alice! That's not nice."

"I know. But those two are scaredy-cats!"

"Are not," Will said.

"Prove it," Alice said. "You boys go into the haunted house."

Tim said, "All right," while the twins shook their heads to say, "No."[34] Tim added, "I'll shine my flashlight out the front window when we are inside."[35]

Imogene whispered, "Tim, you can't. It's not right."

Tim winked and the three boys went inside the gate.[36]

Imogene and Alice paced on the sidewalk and ate jelly beans. After a while a light beamed from the window of the house. A few minutes later the boys came through the gate.[37] "You did it," said Alice. "We saw your light."

Tim looked surprised.[38] "No," he said. "We were scared. We heard **strange** noises."

"But—we—saw—your—light," Alice said slowly.

"Not **my** light," said Tim. "It doesn't work." He handed the flashlight to Alice. She pushed the button.[39] No light.

"Ohhhh!" screamed Alice. "There is a ghost in the haunted house. I'm getting out of here."[40] She raced away toward her home.

Without a word the grinning twins went up Periwinkle Lane.[41] Imogene and Tim started down the street. "How did you do it?" Imogene asked.

"Easy," said Tim. He opened the flashlight and removed the piece of paper in front of the battery contacts.[42] Now the flashlight worked.[43]

"Won't Alice be surprised when I tell her?" said Imogene.

Tim added, "Yeah, and she won't be calling anyone scaredy-cat any more."

Guideline for Telling the Story

Memorize the first and second paragraphs. The second paragraph gives a clue to Alice's motive for scaring the boys. The paragraph between numbers 16 and 17 gives another clue. Don't memorize the two paragraphs, but be sure to include the clues.

You will want to learn the musical notation for "Who-oo. Who-oo. I'm gon-na get you!" (See Figure 5-1.) Chant the phrase in a spooky voice. A second musical part, "Plink. Plonk. Plinkity, plonk," also needs to be learned. (See Figure 5-2.) Don't worry if you are not a singer. Just chant the phrases as best you can.

This story may take more practice than some of the others because it is longer, but it is one of the children's favorites.

Figure 5-1. Musical Notation

Who-oo / Who-oo / I'm gon-na / get you!

Figure 5-2. Musical Notation

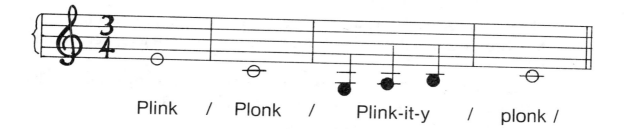

Plink / Plonk / Plink-it-y / plonk /

Outline

I. Will and Bill walk home.
>   A. They talk about the game next week.
>   B. They walk near the haunted house.
>   C. A ghost scares them.
>   D. They run to Tim and Imogene Taylor's house.

II. At the Taylors, Bill and Will explain what happened.
>   A. Imogene teases them about being scaredy-cats.
>   B. Mr. Taylor drives them home.

III. The next evening, Tim and Imogene follow the twins home.
>   A. The ghost jumps out at the twins.
>   B. Bill trips and falls on Will.
>   C. Imogene and Tim chase the ghost.
>   D. The ghost races back toward the haunted house.
>>   1. Tim tries to get the twins to stop the ghost.
>>   2. Imogene shames them into helping.
>>   3. The ghost is Alice.

IV. Alice calls the boys scaredy-cats.
>   A. She dares Tim and the twins to go into the haunted house.
>   B. They promise to shine the flashlight when inside.

V. The girls wait for the signal.
>   A. They see it.
>   B. The boys don't go inside because the flashlight is broken.
>   C. Alice runs home scared.

VI. Tim explains how he fixed the flashlight.

Felt Characters and Props

1. Felt characters: Bill, Will, Tim, Imogene, haunted house, and a two-section ghost that is unmasked to be Alice. Cut out and color both parts of the ghost/Alice. Paste the head of Alice under the ghost section at the tab. Crease along the fold line. After the sections are together, add the felt.

2. A paper clip to hold the flap up on the ghost. After many uses, the flap flops down and reveals the ghost's identity too early.

3. A battery-operated flashlight that works.

4. A small piece of paper to slip under the battery contact of the flashlight.

5. Felt board and stand.

6. Text of the story.

Will

Bill

Tim

Imogene

49

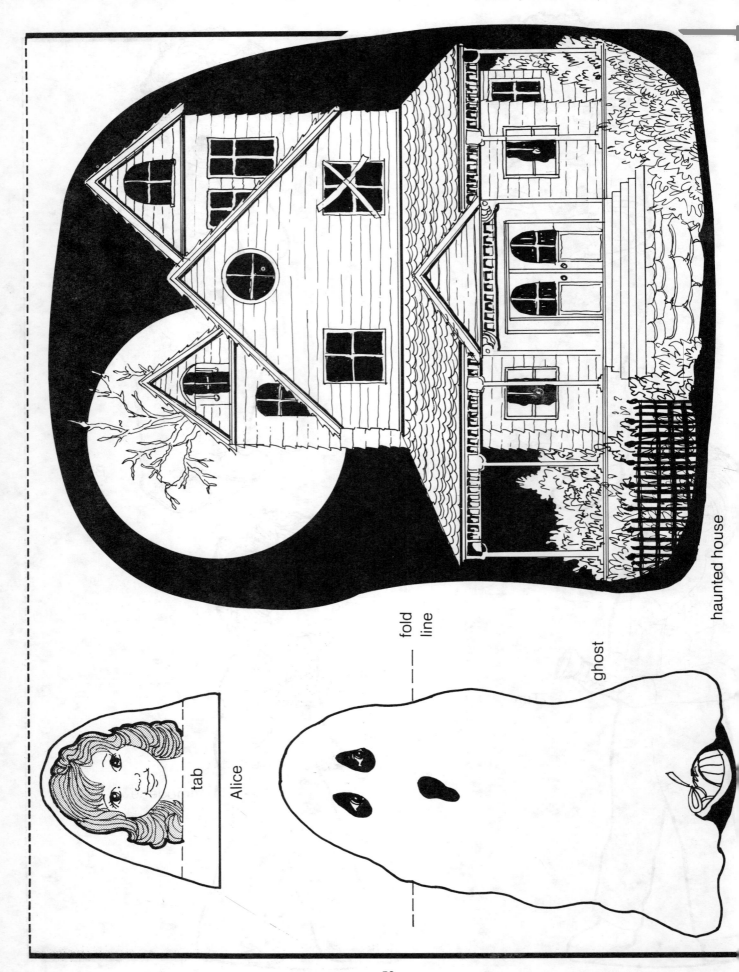

fold
line

tab

Alice

ghost

haunted house

Movements of the Felt Board Characters

Pay careful attention to the movements of the characters and props for "Soccer Spook." Read over the explanations several times and practice the movements. This is a popular story, but clumsy character movements can easily distract eager listeners.

The tale starts with the haunted house in the upper right-hand section of the flannel board. (Directions on the board are always from the audience's viewpoint.) At number 1 place Bill (the one with the B on his shirt) near the middle of the left side. At 2 put Will to the right of Bill. Point to Will at 3. At 4 pick up Bill and move him, as if he is playing leapfrog over Will. Position him on the right side of Will. The boys will appear to be walking across the board toward the right side. At 5 pick up Will. As you say the next sentence, leapfrog Will over Bill, moving them farther to the right. Remember that Bill and Will live to the right of the flannel board past the haunted house. The characters should be nearing the haunted house. If they are not close enough, leapfrog them one more time. At 6 shake your head. Say, "Strange stories!" in a slow, spooky voice at number 7.

At 8 chant the ghost's words in a musical chant. (See Figure 5-1, page 47.) This same chant is used later when the ghost reappears. Look around the room at 9. At 10 pop the ghost onto the board near the haunted house. Pick up Bill and Will in one hand at number 11 and rush them across the board from the right side to the left. Temporarily put the twins down. Remove the ghost and the haunted house, preferably taking them off to the right side of the board. We don't want them chasing the twins, yet.

Place Bill and Will in the center of the board as you begin the second section of the story. At 12 put Tim next to the twins. At 13 position Imogene nearby. Point to Imogene at 14. At 15 remove all the flannelgraphs from the board. Shake your head to emphasize "no such things as ghosts" before number 16.

The third part begins with the board blank and remains blank through the paragraph. At 17 place the haunted house in the upper right-hand corner of the board. At 18 put the twins, followed by Tim and Imogene, on the left center of the board.

Move the four characters toward the right side of the board where the haunted house sits by leapfrogging the twins, then leapfrogging Tim and Imogene. Pause for the movement. Be sure to use the same musical chant as before for the ghost. At 19 pop the ghost out from the right side of the board and put it below the house. Really scream, "Ahhh," at 20. At 21 place Bill and Will tipped on their sides next to each other. They should be slightly to the left of the haunted house.

At 22 pick up Imogene and Tim in one hand and jump the twins. Then move the ghost down and to the left in a clockwise motion, putting it back on the board at the left side. At 23 move the Taylors down and to the left in a clockwise motion and place them just below the ghost. Pick up the ghost and move it in a circular motion clockwise around the edge of the board. End the motion by placing the ghost in the lower center. The ghost has made a revolution and one quarter in the last two moves. At 24 make a large circle with the Taylors. End their revolution by placing them in the lower left-hand section. At 25 move the ghost slightly toward the house.

"Plink. Plonk. Plinkity, plonk" at 26 and 27 should be sung as in Figure 5-2, page 47. The chant could be repeated several times. At 28 set Bill upright. Back up the twins at 29, by moving them slightly to the right. In the process, put Will on his feet again. At 30 stretch out your arms. At 31 close your eyes tightly. Open them at the end of the sentence. Move Tim and Imogene up and right beside the ghost at 32. At 33 take off the paper clip on the ghost flannelgraph. Bend down the flap to reveal Alice.

At 34 shake your head from side to side. At 35 pull out a flashlight. Do not try to turn it on since it has been fixed not to light. Remove Tim, Bill, and Will at 36. Put the flashlight down behind the flannel board. Put the flannelgraphs for Bill, Will, and Tim next to Alice and Imogene at 37. At 38 reach back and get the flashlight. At 39 turn on the flashlight. It shouldn't work. At 40 race Alice off to the left. At 41 slide the twins off to the right. Remember that the twins live to the right of the flannel board past the haunted house.

While you say sentence 42, open the flashlight and remove the piece of paper in front of the battery contacts. Screw the flashlight back together. At 43, turn the flashlight on. The story ends with Tim and Imogene on the felt board alone and the flashlight in your hands.

Hints

"Soccer Spook" is a good story for any time of year since most cities have soccer season continually.

Precede the story with the question, "Do you like to figure out mysteries and puzzles?" Most of the children will say "Yes." Tell them that this is their chance to try to solve two mysteries, but warn them not to say anything until the story is over. Otherwise they might spoil someone else's chance to figure it out themselves.

After the story, ask them how many knew ahead of time who was the ghost. Ask them what clues led them to think that. Then ask them how many knew how Tim made it look like he was inside the haunted house. Ask how many knew how he fixed the flashlight.

Be prepared. Everyone will want to try the paper trick with the flashlight. Either be willing to let them try or hide the flashlight immediately after the story.

Suggestions for Language Development, Discussion, and Creative Activities

Science Experiments: In the story the paper blocked the flow of the current in the flashlight. Kindergartners could easily understand this concept. Have them stand in a circle holding hands. Unlink one set of hands to show the break in current. First and second graders could expand the concept by experimenting with simple battery, light, and wire circuits.

Art Activity: Included are sheets to duplicate for each child. The children can color the characters, paste them on a light cardboard, and cut them out. They can tape Popsicle sticks to the backs to make stick puppets.

Language Development: Discuss what roles dialogue plays in stories. Explain that dialogue helps to move the action along and often shows what is happening. For example, "Here it comes," tells us the ghost is coming toward the twins. Dialogue tells about the character who is speaking by what he says. For example, Will says, "That's their problem." That shows he is not sensitive to the girls' needs. Dialogue can tell about other people. For example, "Alice never gets home from trumpet lessons on time." See if the students can think of other things dialogue can do. (Describe a scene, tell how someone feels.)

Creative Writing: The puppets can be used to write (or prepare verbally) a short dialogue between characters. Some students might want to write a complete play.

Song: A fun chant, "Who Stole the Cookie from the Cookie Jar," is listed in the Resources for a Story Hour section. Position the students in a circle. The person who starts the chant suggests the person to the right as the guilty party. That person suggests the person to his or her right. The guilt is passed around the circle until it returns to the person who started the chant.

SOCCER

SPORT

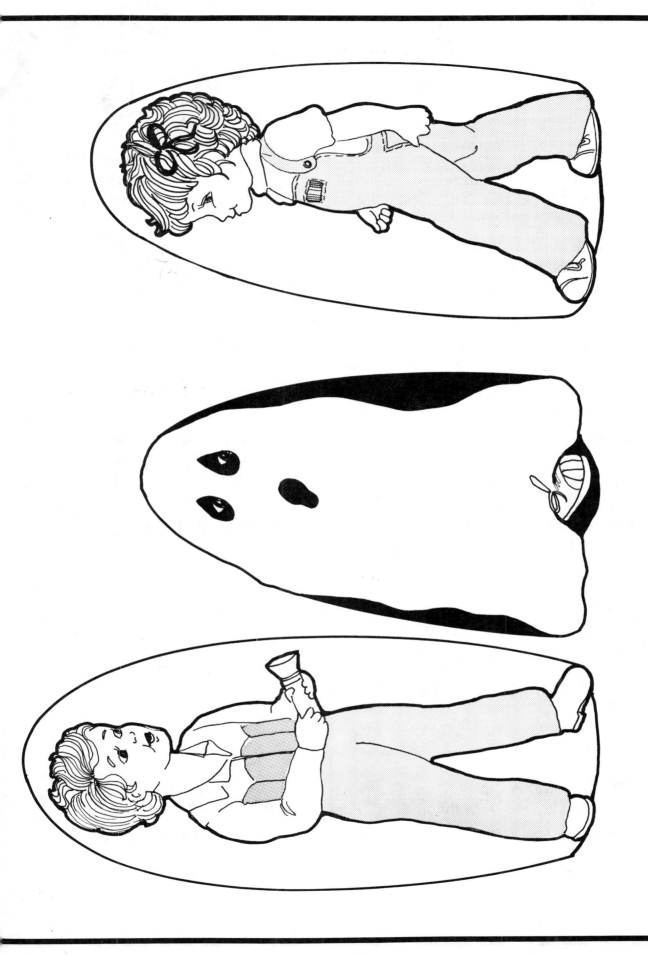

Resources for a Story Hour

Puzzles and Mysteries

Books:

Brian Wildsmith's Puzzles by Brian Wildsmith. Watts, 1970. (Colorful, visual puzzles. Not suitable for large groups because they won't be able to see the details clearly enough.)

Duffy & the Devil: A Cornish Tale by Harve Zemach. Farrar, 1973. (A variant of ''Rumpelstiltskin.'' A longer tale, but delightful.)

It Looked Like Spilt Milk by Charles G. Shaw. Harper, 1947. (What is it? Short.)

Snail, Where Are You? by Tomi Ungerer. Harper, 1962. (A wordless picture book with a spiral hiding on each page.)

Something Queer at the Library by Elizabeth Levy. Delacorte, 1977. (A who dunnit.)

Where Does the Butterfly Go When It Rains by May Garelick. Scholastic, 1961. (Its blue illustrations are difficult for use with a large group because they are so indistinct. Perfect for a small group on a cozy, rainy day.)

Who, Said Sue, Said Whoo? by Ellen Raskin. Atheneum, 1973. (A delightful tongue twister.)

Chants:

''Who Stole the Cookie from the Cookie Jar?'' From *The Wheels of the Bus Go Round and Round* collected by Nancy Larrick. Golden Gate, 1972, p. 8. (Traditional school chant.)

Poems:

''The Mysterious Cat'' by Vachel Lindsay. From *Time for Poetry* compiled by May Hill Arbuthnot. Scott, Foresman, 1952, p. 48.

''Someone'' by Walter de la Mare. From *Time for Poetry* compiled by May Hill Arbuthnot. Scott, Foresman, 1952, p. 136.

Chapter VI

Jingle Bunny

A Participation Story

Once upon a time when the woods sparkled with snow, there was a small bunny named Jingle (xxx).[1] Jingle (xxx) always wore a striped cap with a bell on top so when he hopped, he sounded happy.

On this particular Christmas morning, Jingle (xxx) was taking Christmas presents to his three friends. Last year Jingle (xxx) had four[2] friends to give presents. He thought of his ex-friend, Berny Bunny and then looked at the two cookies in his basket.[3] "It would be nice if he and Berny were friends again," he thought.

But then, Jingle (xxx) thought about the big fight between Berny and himself. Each of them was sure that the other one had led them into the den of the ferocious fox called Flump (fff).[4] They both escaped from the den with scrapes and bruises. Ever since that day ferocious old Flump (fff), the fox with the big floppy feet, licks his lips whenever he catches the scent of Berny or Jingle (xxx). And ever since that day, Berny and Jingle (xxx) were no longer friends.

Jingle (xxx) skipped through the snow carrying his basket. Inside the basket were three wrapped presents and two big Christmas cookies. One was a star-shaped almond cookie[5] and the other was a huge wreath with green icing and red sprinkles on top.[6] If Jingle (xxx) gave the star cookie to Berny, they might become friends again. Jingle (xxx) would still have the wreath cookie for his Christmas day. It was hard for Jingle (xxx) not to take a lick or nibble of the sweet smelling cookie.

Jingle (xxx) jumped up and knocked at the tree of Olivia Owl.[7] Behind a rock he thought he saw a red tail.[8] He gave Olivia her present and hurried on saying, "Merry Christmas."[9]

Jingle (xxx) skidded to a stop at the hollow where Marty Mouse[10] lived. He listened. He thought he heard a muffled sound in the snow. Could it be the fox, Flump (fff)? He looked around and saw no one.[11] A twig cracked, so Jingle (xxx) quickly handed Marty Mouse his present and hopped on.[12]

In seventeen hops Jingle (xxx) was at the tree of Sammy Squirrel.[13] He gave Sammy his little package.[14]

Giving presents made Jingle (xxx) jiggle with joy. He decided to give the extra cookie to his ex-friend. Being a careful bunny, Jingle (xxx) circled before heading to Berny's home.[15] As he crossed his own tracks, he saw something that made him shiver. Behind the bunny tracks were the tracks of a fox. Only Flump (fff) had feet that big.

Jingle (xxx) turned slowly.[16] Behind a snowbank he saw a red tail,[17] two pointed ears,[18] two shining eyes, and a grin of sharp white teeth. It was Flump (fff), and he was flopping his feet quickly toward Jingle (xxx). Jingle (xxx) ran as fast as he could, making his bell ring faster than a bumblebee can buzz. He ran, and he looked back. Flump (fff) was getting closer.

Jingle (xxx) smashed into a tree. The big star-shaped cookie fell out of his basket and onto the snow.[19]

Flump (fff) pounced but missed.[20] Jingle (xxx) scrambled up. Flump (fff) sat in the snow and sniffed the air.[21]

Jingle (xxx) hated to leave the cookie he had decided to give Berny, but he did. He ran as fast as he could right past Berny Bunny's hutch.[22]

Flump (fff) did not chase Jingle (xxx); instead he sat in the snow taking tiny bits of the star cookie—to make it last all day.[23]

Jingle (xxx) looked at his last cookie and then at Berny's house. ''I'll give myself a friend for Christmas instead of a cookie,'' he said. Oh, but it did smell good!

Jingle (xxx) gave Berny[24] the big wreath cookie with green icing and red sprinkles.[25] They became good friends again.

Berny and Jingle (xxx) spent that Christmas day in Berny's hutch sharing tiny nibbles of a huge wreath cookie—so it would last all day. A faint sound flowed from the hutch. It was the tinkle of the bell on the cap of one happy bunny named Jingle (xxx). That bell kept ringing ''Merry Christmas'' all day long.

Guideline for Telling the Story

"Jingle Bunny" is an easy story to tell. Have the text of the story within view, so you remember to stop to do the actions. After becoming familiar with the story, reading it is the best method of telling this story.

Ask the children to help you tell the story. Tell the children to listen for the special words, **Jingle** and **Flump**. Instruct them to shake the bells they have been given (or say "ting-a-ling-a-ling," if no bells are available) when they hear the word **Jingle**. Let them practice once or twice. When you say "Flump," have them slap their legs with their hands seven times.

Outline

I. Jingle is taking presents to his three friends.
        A. He remembers the fight with his fourth friend.
        B. Jingle looks at his three presents and two cookies.
        C. He thinks about giving one cookie to Berny.
II. Jingle delivers presents to Olivia Owl, Marty Mouse, and Sammy Squirrel.
III. Jingle decides to give a cookie to Berny.
        A. He circles and sees fox tracks.
        B. He sees Flump and runs.
        C. Jingle trips and drops star-shaped cookie.
        D. Flump jumps at Jingle, misses, and eats cookie.
IV. Jingle gives his last cookie to Berny.

Felt Characters and Props

1. Felt characters: Jingle Bunny, star-shaped cookie, wreath cookie with **green** icing and **red** sprinkles, Olivia Owl, Marty Mouse, Sammy Squirrel, Flump's tail which is **red**, Flump's head and Berny Bunny.
2. Jingle bells: Several small bells tied to a circle of ribbon make ringing easier. Provide bells for each child. If bells are impossible, substitute the verbal "ting-a-ling-a-ling."
3. The text of the story open if necessary nearby to remind you when to lead the children in the jingling and flumping.
4. Felt board and stand.

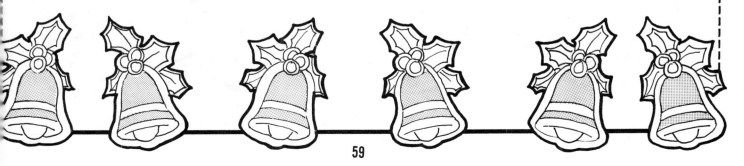

Berny Bunny

star cookie

Jingle Bunny

Sammy Squirrel

Olivia Owl

wreath cookie
green icing, **red** sprinkles

61

Flump with **white** teeth

Flump's **red** tail

Marty Mouse

Movements of the Felt Board Characters

Begin the story with Jingle the rabbit in the center of the board. At 1 and all the other places where "(xxx)" appears, shake some bells or say "ting-a-ling-a-ling." Hold up four fingers at 2. At 3 point to the cookies in the basket. At number 4 slap your knees with your hands five or six times to make a thumping noise. Each time (fff) appears in the text, lead the children in making the thumping noise of Flump's feet. Take the star-shaped cookie from the basket and show it to the children at number 5. At 6 show them the wreath cookie.

At 7 put Olivia the Owl in the upper right-hand corner of the board. At 8 put the red tail at the far left of the board. Leave the tail there while Jingle delivers his presents. Remove Olivia the Owl from the board at number 9.

At 10 put Marty Mouse on the right side of the board. Look around the room as if you were scared of something at 11. At 12 remove Marty Mouse.

At 13 put Sammy Squirrel on the right side of the board. At 14 remove him.

Pick up Jingle and move him in a circle around the board at number 15. Then place him back in the center of the board. Turn your head around slowly as if you fear something is behind you at 16. At 17 point to the tail which has been left on the board since number 8. Add the head to the fox at number 18. CAUTION: Do not try to have the fox chase the bunny on the board. Just keep up the jingling and flumping. At 19 take the star-shaped cookie out of the basket and place it on the felt board several inches away from Jingle. At 20, after finishing the leg slapping, pick up Flump and place him next to the cookie so that the cookie is between Flump and Jingle. Sniff the air at 21. At 22 pick up Jingle and move him off to the right. Pause at 23 before continuing the story. Then remove Flump and place Jingle in the center of the board.

Place Berny to the right of Jingle at 24. At 25 put the wreath cookie between them.

Hints

A Christmas party is a good time for "Jingle Bunny." You can ask your homeroom mothers to provide the jingle bells on ribbons for the children as a special purchase. Children have such fun ringing the bells that extra effort to get bells is warranted.

If you have to provide the bells, be sure to collect them for use next year.

Be sure to let the children try ringing the bells and slapping their legs before the story starts. They will get their most enthusiastic ringing and slapping over with and will not overdo it during the story.

Suggestions for Language Development, Discussion, and Creative Activities

Language Development: Discuss action words (verbs). Ask your students to name action words (words of doing). Give them some examples like **run, jump, sing**. When they can name several verbs, they are ready to play Coffeepot.

The player who is "it," whispers an action word to you. This insures that the word is a verb. "It" starts by saying a sentence that uses the verb, but he or she substitutes the word **coffeepot** for the action verb. For example, "I like to coffeepot" instead of "I like to sing." The other players take turns asking questions, always substituting the word **coffeepot** for the unknown verb. For example, "Do goldfish coffeepot?" "It" would answer, "No, goldfish do not coffeepot." The players ask questions until ready to guess what the verb is. The player who guesses thinks up the next verb.

Creative Thinking: Put the group in a circle. Explain that everyone must give one answer in turn. No one can skip a turn. Tell them you will give them five mintues, and you will keep a score. You will give them one point for each answer. You will give three points for a creative or humorous answer. Ask them to name as many kinds of gifts as possible. Answers like toys, clothes, ordinary gifts would get one point. Answers that are not tangible gifts would get three. For example: a kiss, making my bed, a gift horse. Do not keep the score on the board or so they can see it, because it might inhibit their thinking. At the end of five minutes stop them and give them their scores.

Song: A story time is a perfect time to include Christmas songs. "Jingle Bells" would be even more fun if the children had their bells from "Jingle Bunny" to ring as they sing.

Creative Writing: Talk about the many different types of cookies there are. Ask your students to pretend that they are the baker for the famous king of Kicketoo. Have them write stories about the official cookie of Kicketoo. What would they name the cookie? What would the cookie look like? What would it taste like? What would it be made of? How would the baker serve it?

Books:

The Christmas Totem by Viktor Rydberg. Coward, McCann & Geoghegan, 1981. (A longer book with a serious tone.)

How the Grinch Stole Christmas by Dr. Seuss (Theodor Seuss Geisel). Random, 1957. (This wonderful tale delights all ages.)

The Little Drummer Boy by Ezra Jack Keats. Collier Books, 1972. (Popular song with beautiful color pictures. The music is also given.)

Mouskin's Christmas Eve by Edna Miller. Prentice-Hall, 1965. (Colorful and gentle story.)

The Night Before Christmas by Clement Moore. Holiday, 1980. (The traditional poem with color illustrations.)

Songs:

''Jingle Bells.'' From *The New Golden Song Book*. Golden Press, 1963.

Poems:

''Best of All.'' From *Cricket in a Thicket* by Aileen Fisher. Charles Scribner's Sons, 1963, p. 43.

''Christmas'' by Marchette Chute. From *Read-Aloud Poems* compiled by Marjorie Barrows. Rand McNally, 1957, p. 62.

''Christmas,'' a Mother Goose rhyme. From *Time for Poetry* compiled by May Hill Arbuthnot. Scott, Foresman, 1952, p. 170.

Filmstrips:

The Bear's Christmas by Stan and Jan Berenstain. Paratone, 1977. (90 frames.)

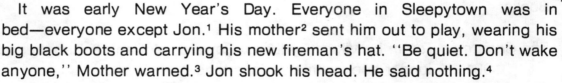

Chapter VII

Jon's New Year's Morning*

It was early New Year's Day. Everyone in Sleepytown was in bed—everyone except Jon.[1] His mother[2] sent him out to play, wearing his big black boots and carrying his new fireman's hat. "Be quiet. Don't wake anyone," Mother warned.[3] Jon shook his head. He said nothing.[4]

He skipped to the north side of the little town.[5] He put on his silver fireman's hat.[6] The rays of the rising sun hit his hat. Reflections danced all over town like an explosion of fireworks.

A ray of light bounced into the window of Mr. Puff.[7] He rolled out of bed and looked out the window. He was wearing his polka-dot pajamas. The reflections from the hat sent rainbow colors flying helter-skelter. Red danced for Mr. Puff. Orange leaped. Gold jetted into the sky. White wiggled and squiggled, then disappeared. "Look, Mrs. Puff. Wake up! Something wonderful is happening. Look outside. Call Dorothy and Aunt Jane," Mr. Puff was shouting. Where were the beautiful colors coming from? He did not know.[8]

Jon hopped to the east side of town.[9] His hat sent the morning sun's rays skittering. They skipped over the frosty grass, through the bare trees, all around Sleepytown. A golden ray slid into the crack in old Mr. Digger's shades.[10] "My goodness! My stars!" he said. He sprang from his bed. His gray beard and wise old eyes peeked from beneath the quilt he wrapped around him. "My! My!" He ran to the telephone. Where did the sparkling come from? He did not know.[11]

Jon jumped, just like a kangaroo, to the south side of Sleepytown.[12] He was careful to be very quiet. With each jump, lights danced. Colors reflected from his silver fireman's hat. The dazzling lights woke up Mayor McPride,[13] Dr. Better,[14] and the Reverend Good.[15] Where did the rays come from? They did not know.[16]

Then Jon ran to the west side of town.[17] As he ran, the rays danced faster. He was having fun playing fireman. He made no sounds. The people of Sleepytown could sleep late today. When a shimmering blue-orange ray tickled Madame Future's eyes, she sat up.[18] The gypsy fortuneteller wore blue curlers in her hair. "A miracle! A sign!" She looked all over, but she could not tell where the rays came from.[19]

Jon took off his silver fireman's hat.[20] He was through playing fireman. He walked to the park in the center of town.[21] He was quiet. The people of Sleepytown wanted to sleep late today.

But everyone in Sleepytown was in the park.[22] "Did you see it?" Mr. Puff asked.

*First published in *Children's Playmate Magazine*, 1980, Indianapolis, Indiana.

"My! My! My!" old Mr. Diggers kept saying.[23]

"It's a sign!" Madame Future said.[24] She still wore her curlers.

"Did you see anything extraordinary, Jon?" Major McPride asked.[25]

"No," said Jon. "I played fireman very quietly so everyone could sleep."

"Well, whatever it was," said the Mayor, "it was something wonderful—something special for the New Year."

"Something wonderful will happen this year," Madame Future said. "I just know it." All of Sleepytown agreed something wonderful had already happened to Sleepytown.

Why did the New Year begin so early in Sleepytown? Where did the light come from? No one ever knew. But they all agreed it was going to be a wonderful year.

Guideline for Telling the Story

This story is short and easy to learn. The first paragraph is important for understanding the irony of the story. It should be memorized or learned thoroughly. The last paragraph also could be memorized.

Outline

I. Jon's mother sent him out to play wearing his new fireman's hat.
    A. On the north side of town he awakens Mr. Puff.
    B. On the east side of town the rays awaken Mr. Diggers.
    C. On the south side of town, the rays awaken Mayor McPride, Dr. Better, and Reverend Good.
    D. On the west side of town, the rays awaken Madame Future.
II. Jon takes off his hat.
III. Everyone in the park wonders what made the colors that woke them all up.

Felt Characters and Props

1. Felt characters: Jon; the Hat, which is **silver** with **multicolored** rays; Mother; Mr. Puff; Mr. Diggers; Madam Future, whose curlers are **blue**; and the three-person character for Mayor McPride (left), Dr. Better (center), and Reverend Good (right).
2. Felt board and stand.
3. Text of the story.

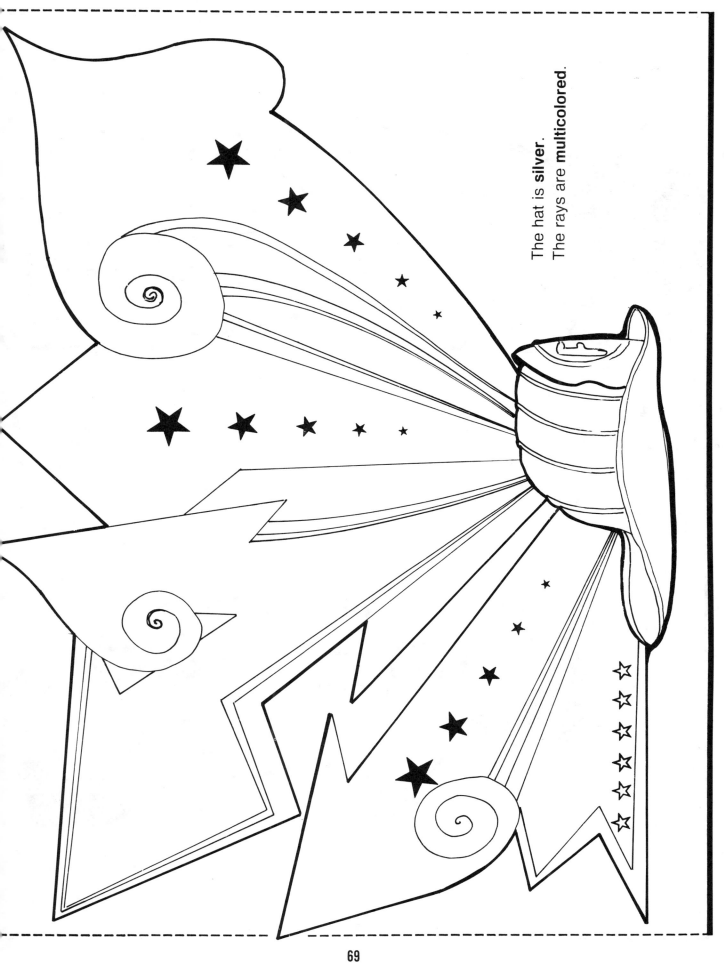

The hat is **silver**.
The rays are **multicolored**.

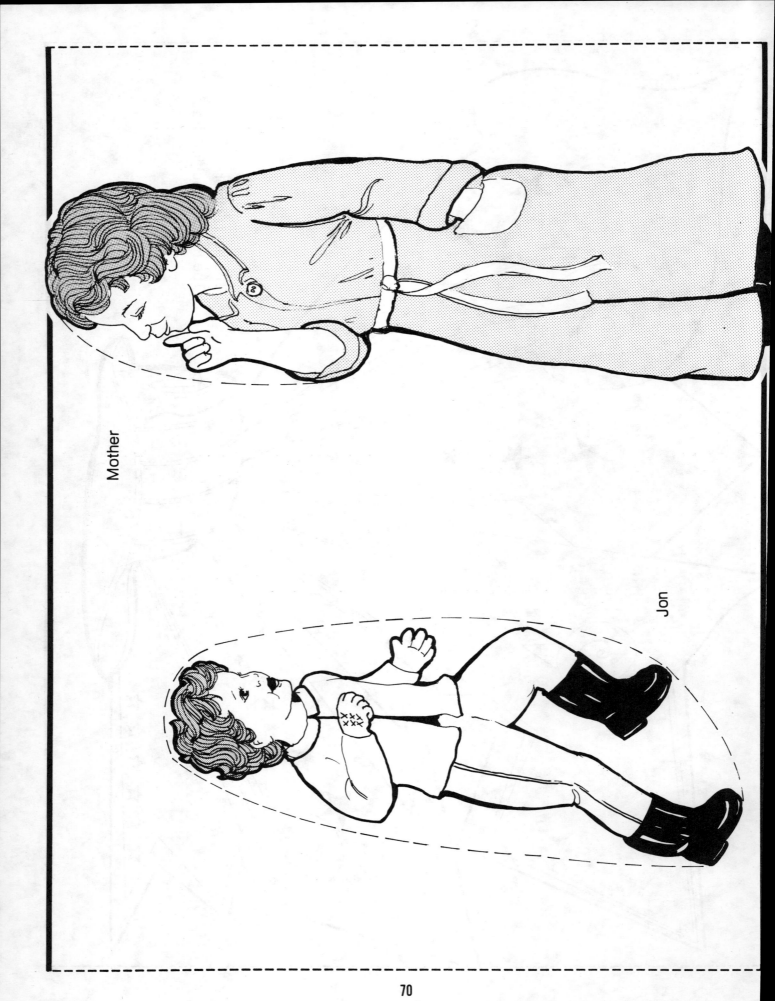

Mother

Jon

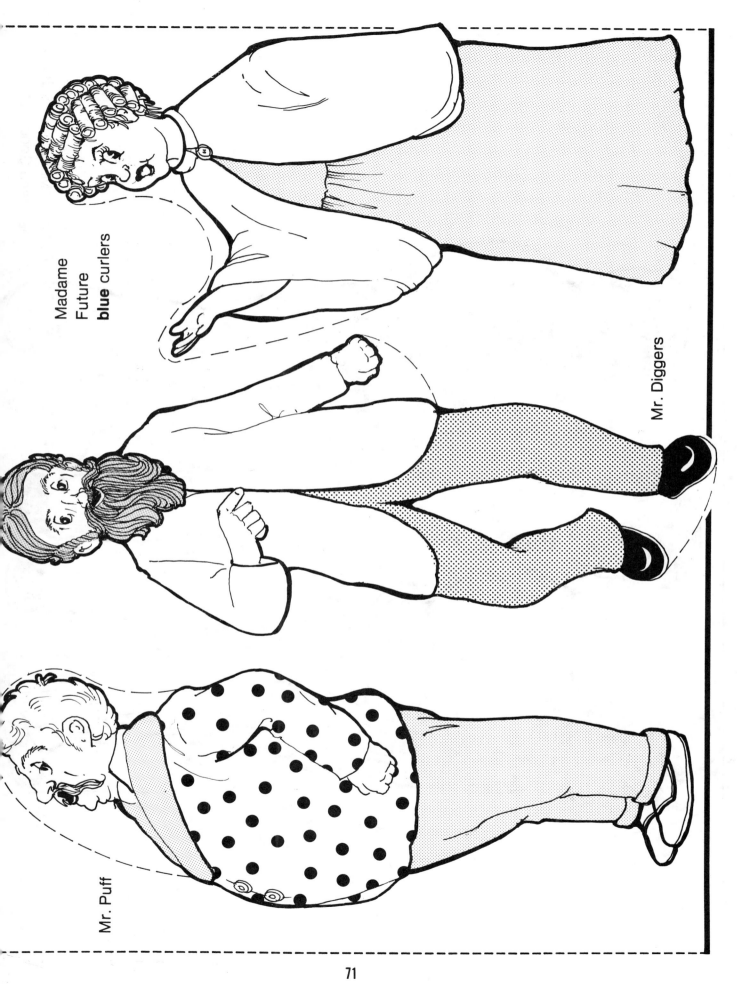

Madame
Future **blue** curlers

Mr. Diggers

Mr. Puff

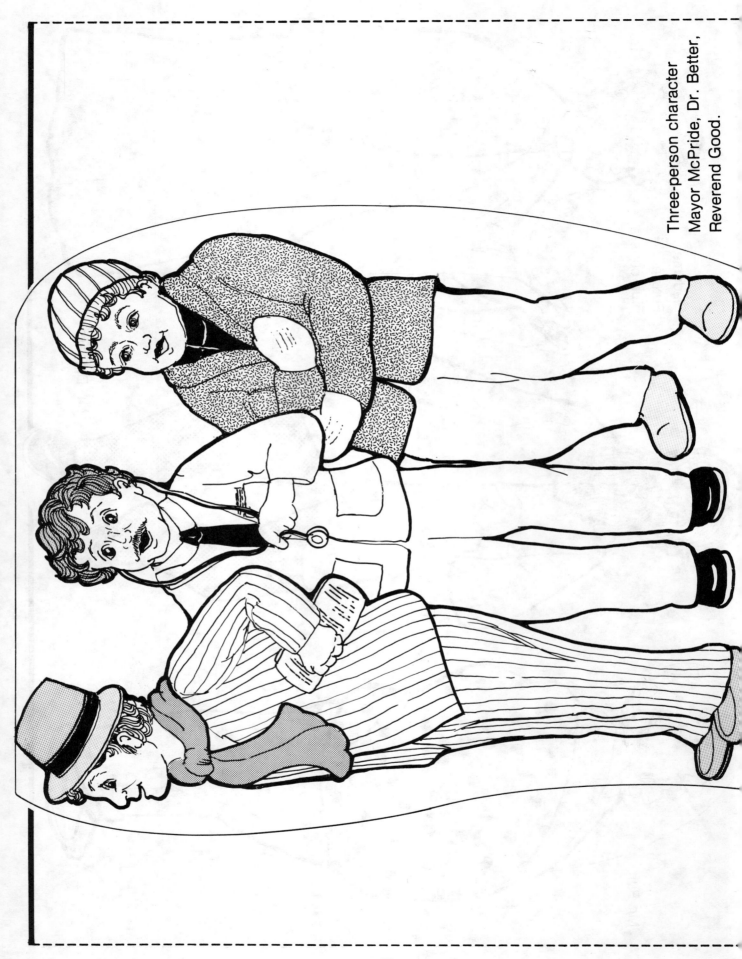

Three-person character
Mayor McPride, Dr. Better,
Reverend Good.

72

Movements of the Felt Board Characters

Begin the story with the felt board empty. At 1 place Jon in the center of the felt board. At 2 place Mother on the board next to Jon. Shake your finger at the children at 3. Remove Mother at 4.

Move Jon to the top of the felt board at 5. The directions (north, east, south, and west) in this story are the same as they would be on a map. At 6 put the hat on Jon's head. Add Mr. Puff at 7 and remove him at number 8.

Move Jon to the right of the felt board (east) at 9. At 10 add Mr. Diggers. Remove Mr. Diggers at 11.

Move Jon and his hat to the bottom of the board (south) at number 12. Add the three-person character at number 13 and point to Mayor McPride (in the top hat). At 14 point to Dr. Better (with the stethoscope); at 15 point to the Reverend Good. At 16 remove the three-person character.

Move Jon and his hat to the left of the board (west) at number 17. Add Madame Future at 18. Remove her at number 19.

At 20, take the hat off Jon, and remove it from the board.

Move Jon to the center of the felt board (number 21). He will remain here until the end of the story. At 22 add Mr. Puff. At 23 add Mr. Diggers. At 24 add Madame Future. At 25 add the three-person character of the mayor, doctor, and reverend. The story ends with Jon in the center surrounded by all the characters except his Mother and the hat.

Hints

"Jon's New Year's Morning" is a good story to tell right after New Year's when children know what it feels like to have to be quiet because adults stayed up too late.

The children need to know what reflections are to understand this story. Show them how sunlight reflects with mirrors, prisms, and a glass filled with water. Let them see the rainbows that refracted light makes.

73

Suggestions for Language Development, Discussion, and Creative Activities

Discussion: Brainstorm with the group to see how many kinds of hats they can think of. Make no negative comments on their responses. Let their creative and off-the-wall responses be accepted. Next ask them to name as many uses for a top hat that they can think of. Encourage them to be creative. ''A banquet table for mice'' would be an acceptable response as well as ''to keep someone's hair dry when it rains.'' This is a lot of fun and is an exercise in creative thinking.

Art Activity: Let your students create hats out of newspaper or construction paper, decorated any way they wish. Ask them to name their hats. Have a parade of hats announcing them as you would a fashion show. Award ribbons for the Funniest Hat, the Prettiest Hat, the Smallest Hat, the Biggest Hat, the Hat Most Likely to Float, the Hat Frankenstein Would Like.

Science Discussion: Since the story deals with reflection and refraction of light, a discussion of light and colors would be appropriate for the older age groups. Experiment with colors by breaking up light into rainbows with prisms. Experiment with mixed colors by using colored films. For example, prove that red and blue when mixed make purple.

I Spy Game: A popular game I Spy encourages children to observe objects and their colors. Choose an object that everyone can see and say, ''I spy something''—and name the color of that object—''green.'' The students take turns guessing until someone names the object that you have chosen. That child then can choose the next object. It is advisable to have the child whisper which object he chose in your ear so the child doesn't change the object or get the color wrong. This game can go on for as long as you wish.

Song: The song ''My Hat It Has Three Corners'' which is listed in the Resources for a Story Hour section would also provide a good event for an activity time.

Resources for a Story Hour

Hats

Books:

Caps for Sale by Esphyr Slobodkin. W. R. Scott, 1947. (A sly tale.)

Jennie's Hat by Ezra Jack Keats. Harper, 1966. (Simple and colorful.)

Herman's Hat by George Mendoza. Doubleday, 1969. (Imaginative and colorful.)

Who Took the Farmer's Hat? by Joan Lexau Nodset. Harper, 1963. (The wind took the farmer's hat.)

The 500 Hats of Bartholomew Cubbins by Dr. Seuss (Theodore Seuss Geisel). Vangard, 1938. (Every time Bartholomew takes off his hat another one appears.)

The Hat by Tomi Ungerer. Parents, 1970.

The Hat That Grew by Bernard Wiseman. Hall, 1967.

Poems:

"Hat" by Shel Silverstein. From *Where the Sidewalk Ends* by Shel Silverstein. Harper, 1974, p. 74.

"Tight Hat" by Shel Silverstein. From *Where the Sidewalk Ends* by Shel Silverstein. Harper, 1974, p. 83.

Songs:

"My Hat It Has Three Corners." From *The Fun Encyclopedia* by E. O. Harbin. Abingdon, 1968, p. 471.

Filmstrips:

Caps for Sale by Esphyr Slobodkin. Weston Woods. (30 frames.)

Old Hat, New Hat by Stan and Jan Berenstain. Paratone Pictures, 1977. (45 frames.)

Chapter VIII

Gus Groundhog*

Gus Groundhog woke up after sleeping all winter in his burrow. At the meeting of the groundhogs last fall, Gus had said that he wanted to be the Groundhog Day groundhog, the one to look for his shadow on Groundhog Day. Today he knew why no one else wanted that job. February second was too early to get up from his winter sleep.

Gus yawned, wiggled his small black nose, and stretched his short legs. Maybe he could nap just a little longer.[1] He flopped back down in his nest of grass. But if Gus fell asleep,[2] he might miss the Big Day. Gus had promised to look for his shadow. And promises are for keeping. Besides, the animals depended on him. People did, too.

Gus forced his heavy head up. Gus grumbled sleepily, "Fluttering feather fleas." He felt the pathway with his long whiskers.

Slowly Gus crawled along the upper pathway.[3] After a few steps he stopped to rest. He wanted to put his head down and shut his eyes for one minute. "Better move on," he said to himself. "Better move on." He trudged on until he bumped his head on the end of the upper pathway. "Ouch! Fluttering feather fleas." This tunnel was one that Gus had not finished. Gus turned around and went back down the path.[4]

Last summer Gus had built his burrow with six rooms and many pathways. His home was bigger and better than those of his brothers and sisters. "The best burrow in Bloomer's Meadow," he had bragged. But today he wished he had a simple burrow with one entrance.

Then Gus tried another path.[5] And another.[6] He went to his nest and tried still another.[7] None of the paths ended in the damp lightness of the outside world. Gus was LOST in the maze of his own burrow. He couldn't get out!

Gus lay down. He curled his tail to cover his nose. His eyes started to close.[8] He was almost asleep. "I promised," he said.[9] "I wish I hadn't, but I did."

*First published in *Wonder Time*, 1980, Kansas City, Missouri.

Gus thought, if he could not find the right path he would have to dig his way out. It was the only way out. With his front paws and his sharp, curved teeth he tunneled into the ground.[10] He shoved the dirt under his belly. With his back legs he shoved the dirt behind him. All the work woke him up, a little.

Soon the ground became cold and moist. He must be near the top. At last, he popped his head into the snowy meadow.[11]

Gus sat up on his hind legs and looked around.[12] The sun was pale. The trees were bare. Patches of snow lay on the ground. Gus Groundhog was outside on Groundhog Day—just like he promised.

If he saw his shadow, he was to predict six more weeks of winter. **If** he didn't see his shadow, spring was coming. Gus looked for his shadow. There it was, a blue patch on the snow. Gus leaned to the right;[13] the shadow leaned to the right. Gus leaned to the left;[14] the shadow leaned to the left. Yes, it was his shadow.

Gus must tell the other animals. Brrr. Gus shivered as he ran to the hutch of Berny Bunny.[15] Berny Bunny hopped out to meet Gus. He made tracks in the snow.

''Six more weeks of winter,'' Gus said. ''Keep the little bunnies warm.''

Berny Bunny wiggled his nose and said, ''More winter. Yes sir-ee bob. More winter. Yes sir-ee bob.'' Then he scurried back to his nest.[16]

Gus Groundhog sleepily hurried away to warn the other animals. Brrr. Gus sat up and put his paws on his cold ears. Then he ran to tell Olivia Owl.[17] He tapped on her tree. He tapped again.

''Whooo? Who?''

''It's Gus Groundhog. Six more weeks of winter. I saw my shadow.''

Olivia flew out of her hole in the tree.[18] She perched on a limb. ''I comprehend the probability of such preposterous superstitious speculation. It's preposterous, preposterous,'' said Olivia Owl.

''Yes, Ma'am,'' said Gus. He never understood Olivia.[19]

Next Gus ran to the home of Myrtle Mouse.[20] His feet were cold so he did a one-foot-up and one-foot-down dance as he talked to her. "Six more weeks of winter," he called. "Bundle up for winter."

Myrtle peeked from her nest.[21] "Why thank you all kindly, Mr. Groundhog. You all come back now. You hear? When winter is done, you all come back now and **set** a spell." She waved at Gus.[22]

His job was done. Gus sat up one more time to look for foxes or other enemies. Then he ran to his burrow.[23] He slid down his pathway, and curled up in the soft dry grass.[24]

In less time than it takes to say "Happy Goundhog Day" Gus was asleep and dreaming. He dreamed of the meadow lush with clover, warm with sunshine, and sweet smelling with wild flowers. Gus dreamed of spring.

Guideline for Telling the Story

Careful attention must be paid to learning the first part of the story so that Gus's character comes through. Since Gus is the only character in the first part of the story, his motivations and movements are important. "Fluttering feather fleas" and "best burrow in Bloomer's Meadow" are two phrases to memorize.

It is vital to know the results of seeing his shadow. A shadow means winter. No shadow means spring.

The speeches of Berny Bunny, Olivia Owl, and Myrtle Mouse are fun and easy to memorize. The last paragraph should also be memorized.

Outline

I. Gus wakes up in his burrow, too sleepy to do the job he promised to do.
    A. He goes down upper path to dead end.
    B. He wishes he hadn't built the biggest burrow.
    C. Tries three other paths.
    D. He is lost in his maze and sleepy.
    E. Digs his way out.
II. Outside he looks for his shadow and sees it.
    A. Goes to warn others of six more weeks of winter.
        1. Warns Berny Bunny.
        2. Warns Olivia Owl.
        3. Warns Myrtle Mouse.
    B. Goes back to his burrow and dreams of spring.

Felt Characters and Props

1. Felt characters: Gus Groundhog, Berny Bunny, Olivia Owl, and Myrtle Mouse.
2. Felt board and stand.
3. Text of the story.

Gus Groundhog

Olivia Owl

Berny Bunny

Myrtle Mouse

Movements of the Felt Board Characters

The movements of the felt characters for ''Gus Groundhog'' are simple. Begin the story with Gus Groundhog in the center of the felt board. This spot is his nest. At 1 close your eyes and drop your head as if you were falling asleep. At 2 pretend to be forcing yourself to stay awake.

At 3 move Gus toward the middle right side of the felt board to indicate his traveling along the upper pathway. At 4 move Gus back to the center along the same path he just traveled.

Move Gus to the lower right corner at 5, then return him to the center by tracing his path backwards. At 6 move Gus from the center to the lower left corner and then back. At 7 move Gus from the center to the middle left corner and then back.

At 8 close your eyes and nod your head. At 9 force your eyes open and head up. Begin to move Gus straight up toward the top of the felt board a little bit at a time beginning at number 10. By the time you reach 11, Gus should be at the top of the board.

At 12 look around. Lean to your right at 13, to your left at 14.

Add Berny Bunny in the upper right-hand corner at 15. Remove him at 16. At 17 move Gus to the upper left side of the felt board. At 18 add Olivia Owl. At 19 remove her. Move Gus to the upper right side of the felt board at number 20. At 21 add Myrtle Mouse. Remove her at 22.

Move Gus to the upper center of the board at 23. At 24 slide him down (into his burrow) to the center of the board.

Hints

''Gus Groundhog'' is a story geared for telling around Groundhog Day, February 2, but it is effective shortly before and after that holiday.

Before the story begins, tell the children that groundhogs sleep in their burrows underground during the winter. In the spring and summer they run around in the meadows and dig burrows. Many children may not know what a burrow is. Explain that a burrow is an underground nest with several tunnels and usually two entrances. You might draw a picture of a burrow on the chalkboard so they can see how it might look.

Explain that the legend of the groundhog as a weather forecaster is a type of folklore that has been passed down from one generation to another. It is not scientific but only a story told for fun.

Suggestions for Language Development, Discussion, and Creative Activities

Language Development: Ask the children why Gus decided to keep his promise to go above ground and look for his shadow. Ask them why he built a burrow with so many pathways. Ask them why he wished he hadn't promised to be the Groundhog Day groundhog. Ask them why he dreamed of spring.

Motivation is an important element in stories. Explain that why someone does something tells us something about that person. Ask them why someone might help a neighbor rake his leaves. See if they can come up with several different motives. See if they can think up motives for Johnny yelling at the top of his lungs, Tina crying, Mr. Yong limping, or Ms. Martin scolding her students.

Creative Writing: Cut out enough pictures from magazines for each child to have a picture. Ask the child to write a story telling what is happening and **why**, the motive behind the action. Pictures with people in them are usually more effective, but children also can create unusual stories about why no one is around.

Science Discussion: This story is a natural bridge into discussions about groundhogs and their hibernation. Several of the books listed in the Resources for a Story Hour could provide additional information for interested children.

What's Missing Game: Put several small objects on a desk—a pencil, paper clip, comb, eraser, scrap of paper, piece of chalk, etc. Let the children look at the desk. Have them close their eyes. Remove one or more of the objects. Have the players open their eyes and guess what is missing.

Resources for a Story Hour

Groundhog Day

Books:

This Is the Day by John Hamberger. Grosset, 1971. (Animals of the forest go to the meadow to see what will happen on Groundhog Day. Simple and enjoyable.)

Time for Jody by Wendy Kesselman. Harper & Row, 1975. (Nice story with pen and ink illustrations about a groundhog and spring.)

Woodchuck by Faith McNulty. Harper & Row, 1974. (A science ''I Can Read'' book. Nonfiction with color pictures, 64 pages. Not for the youngest listeners. Useful for a group or individual readers.)

Poems:

''How Much Wood Would a Woodchuck Chuck.'' From *Time for Poetry* compiled by May Hill Arbuthnot. Scott, Foresman, 1952, p. 109.

''The Jolly Woodchuck'' by Marion Edey and Dorothy Grider. From *Time for Poetry* compiled by May Hill Arbuthnot. Scott, Foresman, 1952, p. 57.

''Woodchuck.'' From *I Wonder How, I Wonder Why* by Aileen Fisher. Abelard-Schuman, 1962. (unpaged)

Chapter IX

Valentine Kite[*]

Eddie had made a valentine kite[1] for his best friend, Tara. The kite was red and heart-shaped. Eddie wrote, ''BE MINE,'' on it in big black letters. On the day before Valentine's Day, he went to Tara's house.[2]

Tara ran from her porch with her ponytail bobbing up and down like a flag.[3] ''See my new kite,'' she shouted. Then she raced into her backyard. Tara's big box kite sparkled shiny blue and green. Its streamers danced like sunshine on water. Tara ran with her new kite. It leaped; it danced. It flew high into the sky.

''Wow,'' said Eddie. ''What a kite!''

Tara asked Eddie, ''Do you want to fly the best kite ever?''

''No,'' said Eddie. He went home.[4] He could not give his homemade kite to Tara now. She had a better one.

The next day was Valentine's Day. Eddie took the kite he had made to the park.[5] Eddie flew the valentine kite. At least, the kite would make **him** happy. He ran, and the kite flew high. Eddie skipped and laughed, and the kite whirled and spun.

Eddie ran near the bench where Captain Rigger and Mrs. Rigger were sitting.[6] They were two of Eddie's favorite people. Today Captain and Mrs. Rigger didn't seem very happy. The Captain yawned and stared at the sky. Mrs. Rigger said, ''Uh huh, uh huh, uh huh.''

Eddie ran past them with his homemade kite. When they saw the kite, Mrs. Rigger hugged Captain Rigger. ''Oh, Eddie,'' Mrs. Rigger said. ''You and Captain planned this nice valentine surprise.'' Eddie waved but said nothing. His kite had made his friends happy.[7]

The kite followed Eddie as he ran past Ken and Katy.[8] Ken hid a valentine behind his back. Katy peeked shyly from behind a tree. In her hand was a white envelope for Ken. When Eddie's valentine kite flew by, Ken shouted, ''Look.'' Katy looked up at the kite.

''What a clever idea, Ken.'' She gave Ken the valentine, and he gave her a valentine. It wasn't a planned surprise for Katy, but Eddie would never tell.[9]

Eddie could hear Katy chattering as he ran past Sally.[10] She was a pretty, new girl in Eddie's class at school. Eddie reeled the kite tighter. When the kite passed her, pretty Sally waved at **him**! Eddie felt funny. His face was hot. He waved back.[11]

Eddie flew his kite out of the park, past Tara's house, and down the street to his home. When he pulled on the rough cord, the kite landed on a patch of melting snow. Eddie rolled up the kite to put it away until next year.[12]

[*]First published in *Children's Playmate Magazine*, 1980, Indianapolis, Indiana.

Then Eddie took a valentine card to Tara's house. Tara was sick, so he gave the card to her mother.[13] Her mother said, ''The kite you flew past Tara's window made her very happy. It was a very special valentine surprise.'' Eddie looked up and saw Tara in the window.[14]

Eddie's valentine kite had been special to Captain and Mrs. Rigger, to Ken and Katy, to Sally, and now to Tara. Eddie's homemade, heart-shaped kite that said, ''BE MINE,'' wasn't the biggest, and it wasn't the brightest kite in town. But it was the BEST.

Guideline for Telling the Story

"Valentine Kite" is an easy story to learn and tell. Memorize the first and last paragraphs. The rest follows the order in which the felt board characters appear.

Outline

I. Eddie went to Tara's house.
    A. He saw her new box kite.
    B. He decided he couldn't give her the kite he made for her now.
II. Eddie took the valentine kite to the park.
    A. The kite made Captain and Mrs. Rigger happy unexpectedly.
    B. The kite helped Ken and Katy overcome their shyness.
    C. The kite made Sally smile at Eddie.
III. He went home with the kite past Tara's house.
    A. He took a valentine card to Tara, who was sick.
    B. Tara's mother said the kite he flew by earlier made Tara happy.

Felt Characters and Props

1. Felt characters: Eddie; valentine kite which is **red;** Tara with her box kite. The box kite is **blue** and **green**; Tara in the window; Tara's mother; the Riggers (Captain and Mrs.); Ken and Katy (one character); and Sally.
2. Felt board and stand.
3. Text of the story.

Valentine Kite
red

Be
Mine

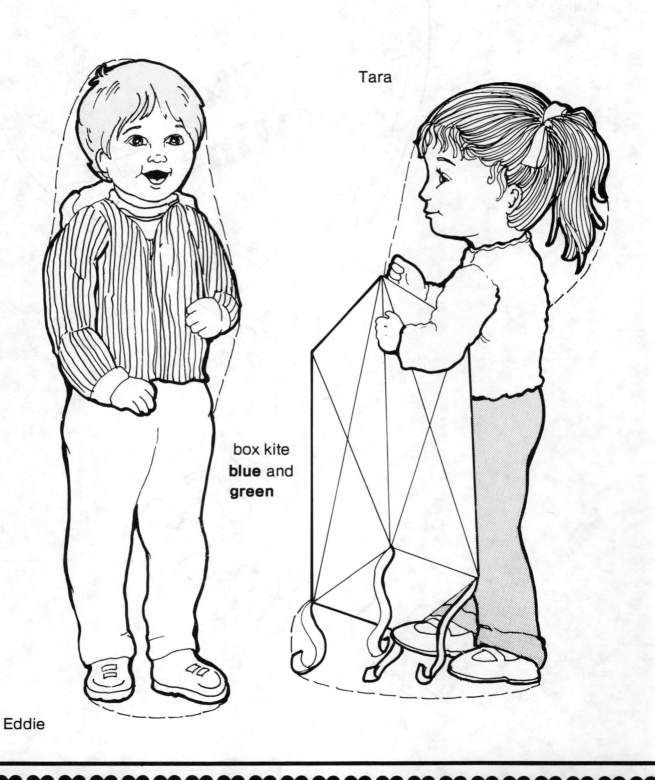

Tara

box kite
blue and
green

Eddie

Ken and Katy

The Riggers

Tara in the window

Sally

Tara's Mother

Movements of the Felt Board Characters

Begin the story with Eddie in the center of the felt board. At 1 add the valentine kite. Remove the valentine kite at number 2. Put Tara with her box kite, next to Eddie at 3. At 4 take off Tara with her box kite.

At 5 put the valentine kite on the board so it looks like Eddie is flying it. Add the Riggers dual character on the right side of the felt board at 6. Remove the Riggers dual character at 7. At 8 put the Ken and Katy double character at the left. At 9 remove Ken and Katy. Put Sally on the right side of the board at 10 and remove her at 11.

Take the valentine kite off the board at 12. At 13 put Tara's mother on the felt board next to Eddie. At 14 put Tara in the window on the board in the upper right-hand corner. Leave the characters where they are as you end the story.

Hints

"Valentine Kite" is a good story to tell around Valentine's Day, although it can be used at other times. Most children, even the littlest, will know about our tradition of expressing our love for someone at Valentine's Day. The most usual expression is a valentine card. Explain that the boy in this story thought of another way to express his friendship.

Suggestions for Language Development, Discussion, and Creative Activities

Art Activity: One natural activity to follow this story would be the making of valentines. Collect wrapping paper scraps, lace, ribbon, macaroni, buttons, pictures from magazines, and yarn to put in a box. Cut out a pattern for a heart. Let the children trace the heart on construction paper and decorate it with the items from the box.

Discussion: Discuss that there are many ways to show your love or friendship for someone. Eddie showed his friendhsip for Tara by making her a valentine kite. See how many ways the children can think of to make someone happy, for example, by giving them a present, by helping them do something, by just being there. Many children find it difficult to discuss feelings, but this question should open up even the shy ones.

Creative Writing: Eddie accidently made many people happy by flying the valentine kite including Tara. Ask your children to write about someone or something that made them feel happy and explain how they knew that they felt happy. Did their toes tingle? Or a smile cross their face?

Song: "Frog Went A-Courtin'" is a popular song with children and is fun to learn. The words and music are in *Frog Went A-Courtin'* by John Langstaff, which is listed in the Resources section.

Tongue Twister: Try out the tongue twister "I saw Esau Kissing Kate" on your class. It is listed in the Resource section.

Resources for a Story Hour

Love

Books:

Arthur's Valentine by Marc Brown. Little Brown, 1980. (Arthur has a secret admirer. Humorous.)

Frog Went A-Courtin' by John Langstaff. Harcourt, 1955. (A Scottish ballad with humorous pictures. The tune is given at the end.)

If You Listen by Charlotte Zolotow. Harper & Row, 1980. (A short, gentle story about love from far away.)

The Valentine Bears by Eve Bunting. Clarion, 1983. (Mrs. Bear wakes Mr. Bear to enjoy Valentine's Day together.)

A Valentine Fantasy by Carolyn Haywood. William Morrow, 1976. (A fairy tale about why hearts are given on Valentine's Day. Slightly longer than the others.)

Poems:

''Hug O' War.'' From *Where the Sidewalk Ends* by Shel Silverstein. Harper, 1974.

''Just Me, Just Me.'' From *Where the Sidewalk Ends* by Shel Silverstein. Harper,1974.

''My Rules.'' From *Where the Sidewalk Ends* by Shel Silverstein. Harper, 1974, p. 74.

''The Turtledoves.'' From *Cricket in a Thicket* by Aileen Fisher. Charles Scribner's Sons, 1963, p. 24.

Tongue Twisters:

''I Saw Esau Kissing Kate.'' In *Tongue Tanglers* by Charles Francis Potter. The World Publishing Company, 1962.

Filmstrips:

Frog Went A-Courtin' by John Langstaff. Weston Woods. (29 frames.)

Chapter X

Grandma's Happy Hat*

It was a warm, windy day. Grandma Dooling was on her front porch, looking in her old trunk. She found a red felt hat.[1] She shook it.[2] The gold bell on it jingled. Should she keep the hat? Should she give it away? A big gust of wind took the hat. It blew the hat right out into the yard.

"Oh, well," said Grandma Dooling, "I'll pick it up later."[3]

But the hat did not stop there. The wind blew it on down the street.[4] It flew into a tired mail carrier who was trudging down the road.[5] Kersmack! He picked up the hat and laughed. When he was a boy, he had owned a hat like it. He put the little hat on his big, bald head. He whistled as he delivered the mail. He sniffed pink carnations as he passed them. He tipped the hat to a boy in a little red wagon.[6]

Suddenly the wind caught the hat and blew it down the street[7] past Tommy[8] and his dog, Thump.[9] They were sitting on the steps doing nothing.

Thump jumped up at the hat. He chased it down the street. Tommy chased Thump. They ran, splashing through puddles and jumping over flower beds. They stopped, laughing and panting by the school yard. Tommy hugged his dog. Thump grinned with the red felt hat in his mouth. "That was fun!" Tommy said. Thump panted.[10]

When Thump dropped the hat, it jingled.[11] The wind tossed it across the street.[12] There Susan sat alone on a big stone in her front yard.[13] The hat landed at Susan's feet. She picked it up and pulled it down over her eyes. "I'll be a fire fighter," she said. She ran down the street.[14] "Clang! Clang! Whir-rrr."

She skipped over to Mrs. Petunia.[15] Mrs. Petunia was washing mud off her driveway with the garden hose. "May I be the fire fighter? I'll pretend to put the fire out on your driveway," Susan said. Soon Susan had the driveway shiny, wet, and clean. Mrs. Petunia was rocking in the chair on her porch. They both smiled.[16]

The fire fighter's hat blew off.[17] It floated high in the air, dancing and twirling. The wind carried it farther and farther down the street. A robin flew at the hat. The hat and the bird played tag. The hat moved faster.

It flew right into the carriage of Mrs. Daisy's crying baby.[18] The baby stopped crying. He kicked the hat to make the bell on the hat ring.[19] Ring-jing-jing. Ring-jing-jing. The baby cooed and smiled. The more the baby kicked, the more the bell rang.[20] Soon the baby was smiling and fast asleep as the wind rocked the carriage.[21]

*First published in *Wee Wisdom*, 1978, Unity Village, Missouri.

Again the wind began to blow. The hat soared into the air.[22] It circled and whirled. It landed right outside the window of Grandma Dooling's house. Grandma came outside.[23] She picked up the hat. She jingled the bell gently.[24]

"Well," she said. "I will keep the hat. It makes me smile. Who knows? Maybe I could find someone it will make happy."

She put the red felt hat back in the old trunk. As she closed the lid, she said, "Little things like this hat can make people happy."

Guideline for Telling the Story

This is an easy story to learn. Once the order of the characters is learned—mail carrier, Tommy and Thump, Susan and Mrs. Petunia, and baby—it is easy. Memorize the first and last paragraphs so the humor of the story is clear.

Find a bell. The ones used for the Christmas story "Jingle Bunny" will do. Each time the hat moves jingle the bell.

Outline

I. Grandma Dooling is looking at a hat in her trunk.
    A. The wind blows it away.
    B. Grandma plans to pick it up later.

II. Happy hat blows to the tired mail carrier.
    A. It makes him happy.
    B. The wind blows it off his head.

III. Tommy and Thump chase the hat.
    A. They have fun catching it.
    B. The wind blows it across the street.

IV. Susan picks it up.
    A. Susan plays fire fighter and washes off Mrs. Petunia's drive.
    B. The hat blows off.
    C. A robin chases it.

V. The hat lands in the baby carriage of a crying baby.
    A. The baby stops crying and kicks the hat.
    B. The hat blows again.

VI. It lands in Grandma Dooling's yard.
    A. She picks it up.
    B. She puts it back in the trunk.

Felt Characters and Props

1. Felt characters: Grandma Dooling, **red** happy hat, mail carrier, Tommy, Thump the dog, Susan, Mrs. Petunia, and the baby carriage.
2. Bells to jingle.
3. Felt board and stand.
4. Text of the story.

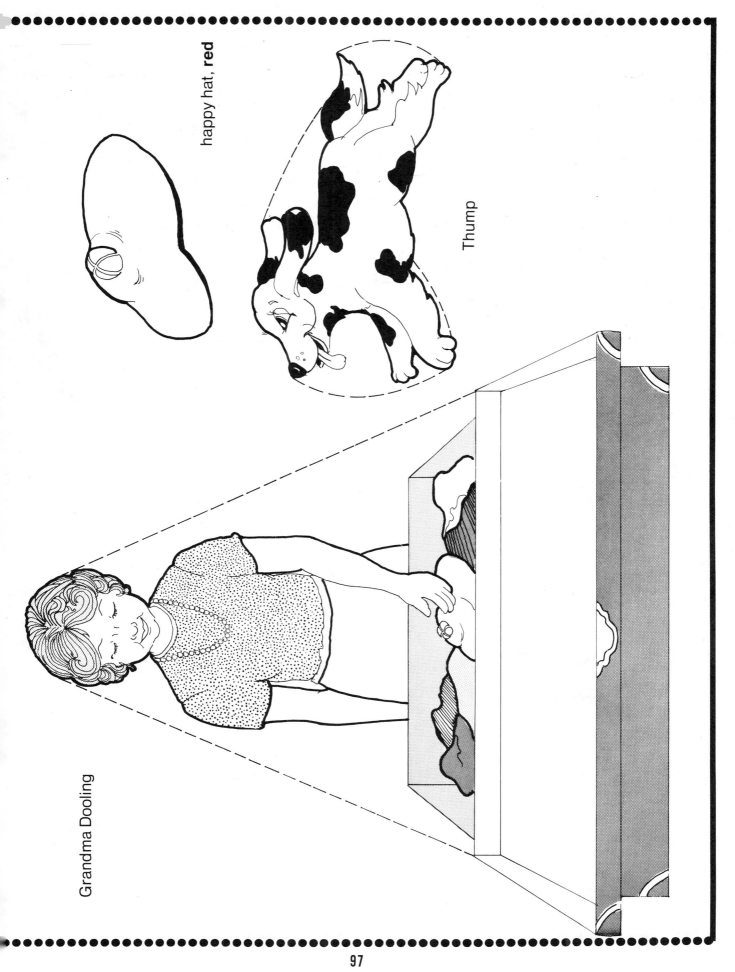

happy hat, **red**

Thump

Grandma Dooling

97

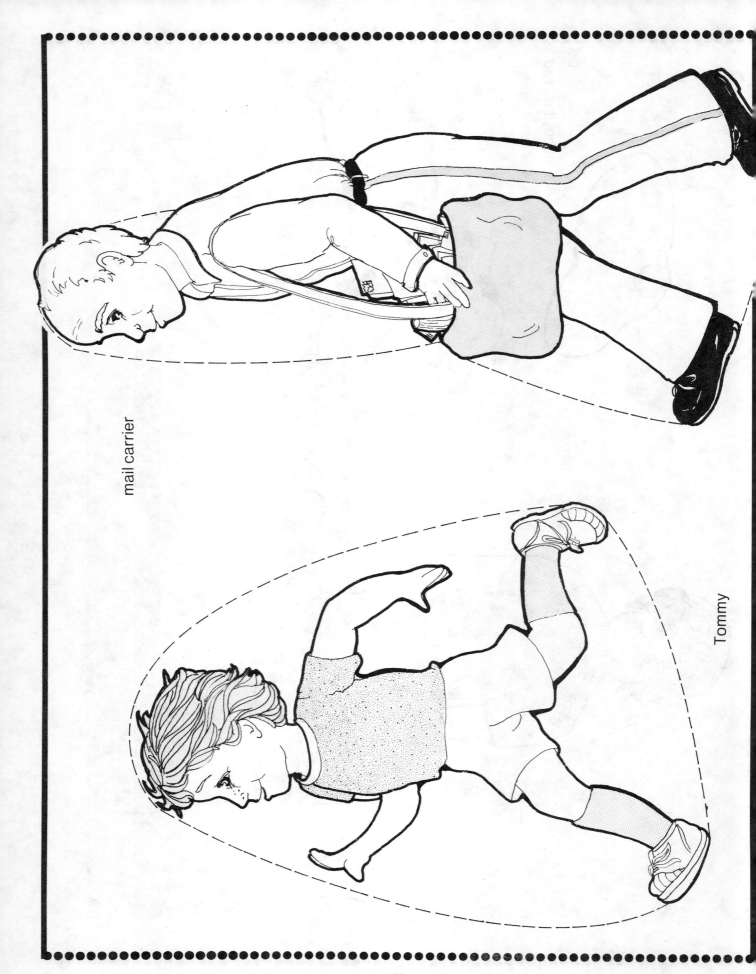

mail carrier

Tommy

98

baby carriage

Susan

Mrs. Petunia

Movements of the Felt Board Characters

Begin the story with Grandma in the upper right-hand corner of the board. At 1 put the hat next to Grandma. At 2 jingle the bell. Remove Grandma at number 3.

At 4 pick up the hat and move it to the left near the top center of the board. At 5 put the mail carrier in the upper center of the board, just to the left of the hat. Remove the mail carrier at 6.

Move the hat near the upper left-hand corner of the board at 7. A little to the left of the hat add Tommy at 8. At 9 add Thump near Tommy. At 10 remove Tommy and Thump.

Jingle the bell at 11. At 12 move the hat to the lower left-hand corner. At 13 add Susan next to the hat. At 14 move Susan slightly to the right. Add Mrs. Petunia to the right of Susan at 15. Remove Susan and Mrs. Petunia at 16.

Pick up the hat at 17, and draw a few loops in the air with the hat during the next few sentences. Land the hat near the lower right-hand corner. At 18 add the baby carriage just below the hat. At 19 begin ringing the bell. Keep ringing it until number 20. Remove the baby carriage at 21.

At 22 pick up the hat and draw a loop in the air and land it in the upper right-hand corner of the board. The hat has made a complete counter-clockwise circle. At 23 add Grandma Dooling. At 24 jingle the bell. The story ends with Grandma Dooling and the hat in the right-hand corner.

Hints

This story is especially good to tell in March or another windy season.

Ask the children if their mothers or grandmothers have some old boxes or big suitcases, like trunks, where they keep things they don't know whether they need to keep or not. This will explain to them what a trunk is.

Ask the children what things the wind blows around. They will probably come up with kites, paper bags, and leaves. Then tell them that this is a story about a hat that the wind blows around.

Suggestions for Language Development, Discussion, and Creative Activities

Science Activity: Discuss the things that the wind makes go like wind generators, kites, windmills, sailboats, and hang gliders. Explain how the shapes of these items use the wind to make them go. Make a simple pinwheel from a square piece of paper, a stick and a pin. (See Figure 10-1, page 102.) See how it traps the wind when you blow at it.

Find the Matching Hats: Copy the activity sheet (page 103) for each child. Have children find the hats that are **exactly** alike.

Creative Writing: In Oklahoma the old settlers say, "If your hat blows off, don't chase it. Just wait for the next one that blows along." Pretend a hat blows to you. It can be any kind of hat. Write a story telling what could happen to you because of that hat.

Song: "If You're Happy and You Know It" is a fun song for any age group, especially with the motions. It is listed in the Resource section.

Language Development: Some words sound like what they describe. Other times, writers make up words to sound like sounds. **Woosh** sounds like something being pushed along by the wind. **Crash** sounds like the noise something makes when it falls. **Hiss** sounds like the noise geese make. Ask the students what kind of noise these words make: **whirr, br--ring, ticktock, thwack, crackle, pop, buzz, squawk, yowl, yap**. See if they can make up any words to describe the following sounds: the bubbling in a glass of water when you blow into a straw, the scratching of a fingernail on the chalkboard, and thumbing through a thick book. Try to get them to come up with new words to describe those sounds instead of repeating ones they know.

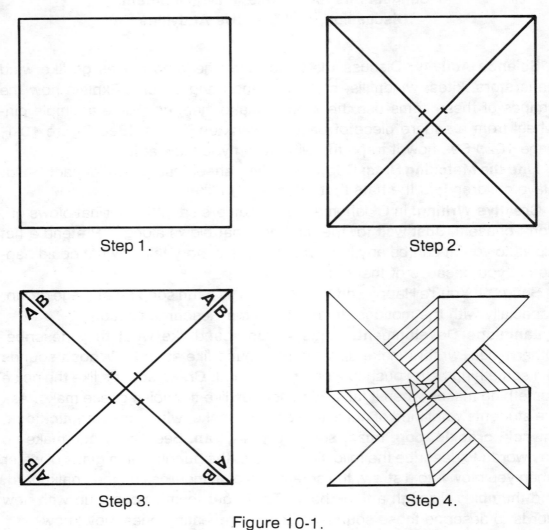

Step 1.

Step 2.

Step 3.

Step 4.

Figure 10-1.

Making a pinwheel

Step 1:   Take a square piece of paper.

Step 2:   Fold the square in half, matching opposite corners. Unfold the square. Fold the square in half a second time matching the opposite two corners. You now have fold lines that form an X on the square. Mark along the four lines 1 inch from the center. Cut along the four fold lines from the corners of the square to the marks.

Step 3:   Label the angles on the outside of the square clockwise **A B A B A B A B.**

Step 4:   Take all the angles labeled **B**. Bring them to the center of the square, overlapping slightly and secure the pinwheel with a pin in the center. Attach the pinwheel to a pencil or small stick.

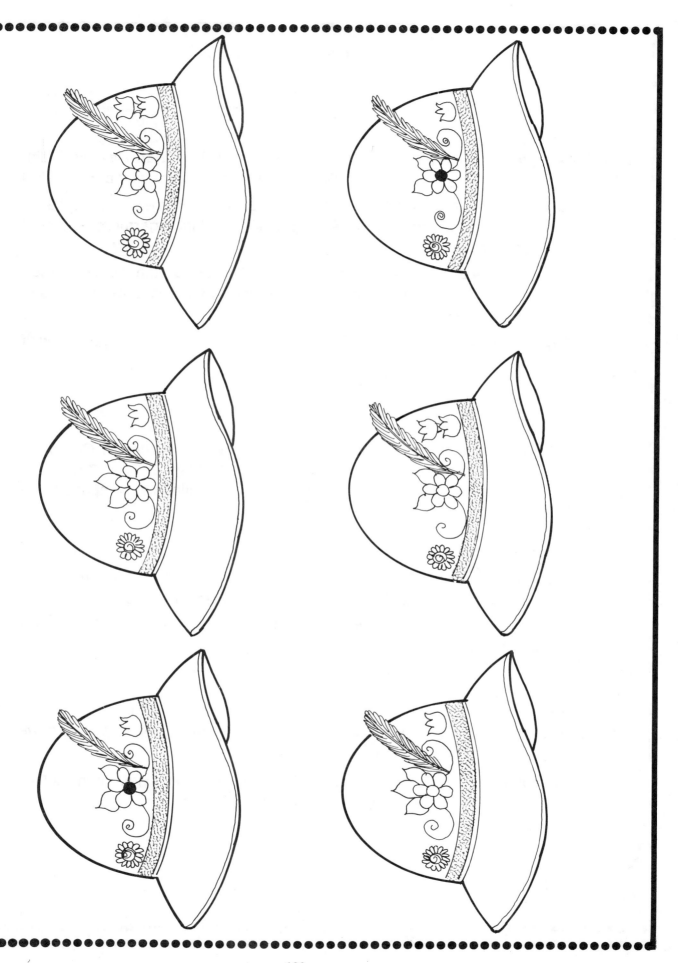

Resources for a Story Hour

Feelings

Books:

Alexander and the Terrible, Horrible, No Good, Very Bad Day by Judith Viorst. Atheneum, 1978. (Black and white drawings and a good tale.)

Do You Know What I'll Do by Charlotte Zolotow. Harper & Row, 1958. (Reassuring story of love, especially for kindergartners and first graders.)

I'm Going on a Bear Hunt by Sandra Stroner Sivulich. Dutton, 1973. (A traditional tale of bravery and fear. Illustrated by Glen Rounds. Motions to accompany the story are given.)

Katy Rose Is Mad by Carol Nicklaus. Platt & Munk, 1975. (Humorous view of anger.)

Songs:

"If You're Happy and You Know It." From *The Wheels of the Bus Go Round and Round* collected by Nancy Larrick. Golden Gate, 1972, p. 20. (Popular group song about many feelings. Motions accompany text.)

Records:

"I Whistle a Happy Tune" by Richard Rogers and Oscar Hammerstein. From the musical *The King and I*. Capital Records, 1956.

"Tomorrow." From the musical *Annie*. Columbia Records, 1977. (A song about hope.)

Poems:

"The Land of Happy" by Shel Silverstein. From *Where the Sidewalk Ends* by Shel Silverstein. Harper, 1974, p. 143.

"Nicholas Grouch." From *Alligator Pie* by Dennis Lee. Houghton Mifflin, 1975, p. 41. (A poem about a grouch.)

Chapter XI

Bungling Prince Botchit (uh-oh) and the Dangerous Dragon (tap, tap-tap-tap)

A Participation Story

Once upon a time the children of Bogan played in the daisy-covered meadows outside their walled city. The merchants sold their spectacles to the people in nearby towns. The people were happy and prosperous. Gentle Prince Botchit (uh-oh)[1] was the town's best maker of glasses. He was the oldest son of the king and soon would be the new king.

One day Prince Botchit (uh-oh) heard a cry at the city gates. "Open the gates. Where are the friendly people of Bogan?"

Prince Botchit (uh-oh) raced to the gate.[2] He tugged at the wooden doors of the city to let in Princess Begonia (wow-wee)[3] from the nearby land of Logis.

Princess Begonia (wow-wee) wore a dress that fluttered in the morning breeze. She felt a warm blast of air on her back. The ground rumbled. Behind her she saw the Dangerous Dragon (tap, tap-tap-tap)[4] who was dragging his spiked tail over the distant hill. The dragon's squinted eyes looked like slits. He crashed into a tree knocking it down.

Prince Botchit (uh-oh) opened the gate for Princess Begonia (wow-wee) just in time. She had come to buy a new pair of glasses in Bogan.

The Dangerous Dragon (tap, tap-tap-tap) ran at the city. The distant rumble crescendoed to an ear-shattering roar. The ground trembled and quaked. The fire scorched the walls around the gate.

The Dangerous Dragon (tap, tap-tap-tap) wouldn't let anyone in or out of the city. The merchants couldn't sell their spectacles. The children couldn't play in the meadow.[5]

Prince Botchit (uh-oh) thought he would never be king of Bogan now. He was the eldest son of the king, but it seemed he never did anything right except make glasses. He pushed his oversized glasses back up the bridge of his nose. "I can't fight dragons with glasses," he thought.

Prince Terrat,[6] the younger son of the king, directed the repair of the wall. Prince Terrat climbed the stone wall, lifted the heavy stones, and replaced the charred boards with fresh boards.

Prince Botchit (uh-oh) was too weak to lift the mighty stones and too short to hold the tall boards while they were nailed in place. He sat by the well drawing water for the thirsty workmen. He felt useless. He lowered the bucket into the refreshing water. He pulled on the rope to raise the bucket of water. He did not watch what he was doing. The full bucket banged into his nose. He yanked the rope and grabbed his glasses before they fell into the well. The bucket swung and splashed water all over Prince Botchit (uh-oh).

Prince Terrat roared with laughter. ''You are useless,'' he said.

That afternoon the king of Bogan called his sons to the royal chamber.[7] As Prince Botchit (uh-oh) walked through the swinging royal doors, one door swung back, and it walloped Prince Botchit (uh-oh) on his backside.[8] His big glasses tilted crooked on his face. Although he bungled most things, the people of Bogan loved gentle Prince Botchit (uh-oh).

Huge Prince Terrat[9] strode into the royal chamber in battle uniform. He waved his dagger. His bushy beard made him look fierce. The townspeople called him ''Terrat the Terrible'' because he was crafty, mean, and strong. Terrat the Terrible said, ''I can slay that Dangerous Dragon (tap, tap-tap-tap). I will lead the army. If I succeed, I demand to be the next king of Bogan, unless my weakling of a brother wants to try first.''

Prince Botchit (uh-oh) didn't like to fight. He was no soldier. He made glasses. He had an idea . . ., but he was afraid to tell anyone. They would laugh at him. The king decided to send Terrat the Terrible and the army to slay the dragon.[10]

Terrat the Terrible[11] led the army into the daisy-covered field. The band played, and the people waved flags. Terrat the Terrible and the army faced the Dangerous Dragon (tap, tap-tap-tap).[12] The Dangerous Dragon (tap, tap-tap-tap) came closer. Terrat and the army backed up. The Dangerous Dragon (tap, tap-tap-tap) came even closer. And the army and Terrat ran back into the walled city of Bogan.[13]

That night the Dangerous Dragon (tap, tap-tap-tap) terrorized the city. The people woke to the sound of hissing fire and a high-pitched dragon wail.[14]

Everyone was sad when Prince Botchit (uh-oh)[15] announced he was going to fight the dragon **alone**. He told no one what he carried in the green pouch on his belt. Everyone, including Prince Botchit (uh-oh), thought he would never return.

That afternoon Prince Botchit (uh-oh) bravely leaped on his horse. As he did, he became tangled in his silk cape. In his struggle to untangle himself, he slid off the other side of the horse. Tears shone in the villagers' eyes.

Prince Botchit (uh-oh) left the horse behind and walked into the field. At the top of the hill, he took his long, silver sword from its holder. It glittered in the sunlight. Prince Botchit (uh-oh) felt the hot earth quake. He touched the tip of his sword to the ground and waited. He leaned on the hilt of his sword, not only to impress Princess Begonia (wow-wee), who was watching from the tower, but also to stop his knees from shaking.

The Dangerous Dragon (tap, tap-tap-tap) loomed above him.[16] Prince Botchit (uh-oh) grabbed the top of his sword, but he couldn't pull it out of the ground. It was stuck. With all his might he pulled back on the hilt of the sword. The sword bent and snapped back throwing Prince Botchit (uh-oh) at the face of the monster.[17] Prince Botchit (uh-oh) landed on the nose of the Dangerous Dragon (tap, tap-tap-tap). He was eye to eye with the dragon. The Prince reached into the green pouch and brought out a huge pair of glasses.[18] He put them over the eyes of the Dangerous Dragon (tap, tap-tap-tap).

The townspeople held their breath. The Dangerous Dragon (tap, tap-tap-tap) opened his mouth. ''I can see!'' he bellowed looking through the glasses. ''I can see the daisies in the fields and the blades of grass and the tiny birds in the sky.''[19]

Prince Botchit (uh-oh) said, ''I thought you were nearsighted with me. I used to run into things just like you used to do.''[20]

The Dangerous Dragon (tap, tap-tap-tap) was so grateful to be able to see clearly that he never scared the people of Bogan again. As a matter of fact, the Dangerous Dragon (tap, tap-tap-tap) became the friendly messenger for Bogan, delivering their glasses to distant towns. When he wasn't busy delivering or marveling at the clear, tiny things he could see, the Dangerous Dragon (tap, tap-tap-tap) took the children of Bogan for a flight on his back.

Prince Botchit (uh-oh) became king. And of course, Prince Botchit (uh-oh), Princess Begonia (wow-wee), and the Dangerous Dragon (tap, tap-tap-tap) lived happily ever after.

Guideline for Telling the Story

"Bungling Prince Botchit and the Dangerous Dragon" is an easy story to tell because it is a participation story. Learn it in the same manner you learn the other stories. However, have the text of the story within view when you tell it, so you remember to stop to do the actions. After becoming familiar with the story, reading it is the best method of telling this story.

Practice this story aloud and put in the words or actions that the children will join you in. After "Prince Botchit" say, "uh-oh," as if you made a mistake. After "Princess Begonia" say, "wow-wee." After "Dangerous Dragon" slap your thighs with your hands in a rhythm: long, short, short, short. Always do the participation movements and sounds before you move the characters on the felt board.

 **Outline**

I. Prince Botchit hears a cry at the gate.
    A. He lets in Princess Begonia.
    B. The dragon rushes at the gate and terrorizes the town.

II. The townspeople fix the gate.
    A. Prince Terrat directs the repair.
    B. Prince Botchit gets water for the workmen and bumps his nose.

III. The king calls his sons.
    A. Prince Botchit gets walloped with the swinging door as he enters.
    B. Prince Terrat demands to be allowed to fight the dragon.
    C. If Terrat wins, he demands to be the next king.

IV. Prince Terrat leads the army against the dragon.
    A. The dragon chases them back.
    B. Again the dragon terrorizes the town.

V. Prince Botchit goes to fight the dragon alone.
    A. He falls off his horse and decides to go on foot.
    B. He meets the dragon.
    C. He is flung by his sword at the dragon's face.
    D. He pulls out a huge pair of glasses and the dragon can see.

VI. The dragon becomes friendly.

Felt Characters and Props

1. Felt characters: Prince Botchit, Princess Begonia, Terrat the Terrible, the King, the Dragon, big glasses.
2. Felt board and stand.
3. Text of the story.

The King

Terrat the Terrible

glasses

Princess
Begonia

Prince
Botchit

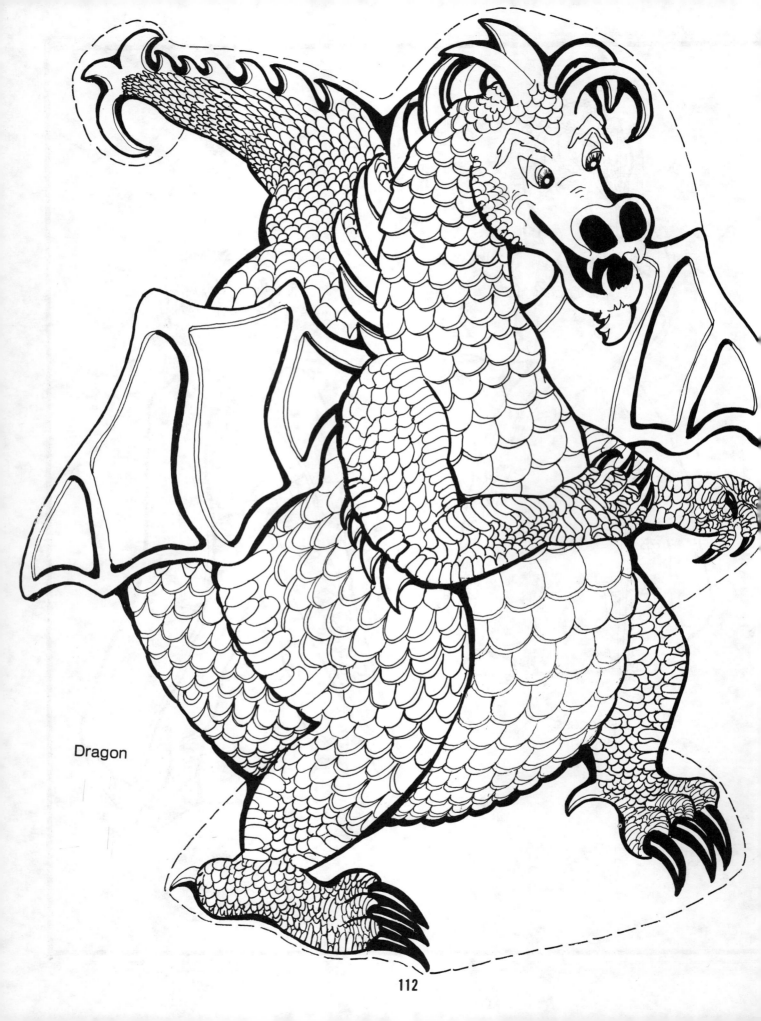

Dragon

Movements of the Felt Board Characters

The movements of this story are simple. Much of the action is told in words with no character movements. Begin the story with the board empty.

At 1 place Prince Botchit in the center of the left side of the board. Move Botchit near the center of the flannel board at 2. Add Princess Begonia at 3 to the right of Botchit. Put the Dangerous Dragon on the right side of the flannel board at 4. At 5 remove the Dangerous Dragon and then Princess Begonia.

Prince Botchit is alone near the center of the board. Add Prince Terrat at 6 near Botchit.

At 7 add the king to the right of the board. At 8 move Botchit from the center toward the king. At 9 move Terrat slightly toward the right. Remove all the characters from the board at 10.

Move Terrat from the left side of the board slightly to the right at 11. At 12 place the Dragon on the right side. Rush Terrat off to the left at number 13. Remove the Dragon to the right at 14.

At 15 place Prince Botchit on the board. At 16 add the Dragon coming from the right side. Pick up Prince Botchit at 17 and land him on the head of the Dragon. The felt character will not stick on top of the Dragon, so place him near the head of the Dragon. At 18 place the big glasses over the eyes of the Dragon. Hold him in place. At 19 place the glasses on the felt board near the top of the Dragon's head. At 20 put Prince Botchit back at ground level. Finish the story with the Dragon, Prince Botchit, and the glasses on the board.

Hints

This story is good any time of the year. Begin the presentation by asking the children to help you tell the story. Have them listen for the special words **Prince Botchit**, **Princess Begonia**, and **Dangerous Dragon**. Instruct them to say, "uh-oh" after they hear "Prince Botchit." When they hear "Princess Begonia" tell them to say, "wow-wee." After hearing "Dangerous Dragon," have them slap their legs with their hands in this rhythm: long, short, short, short. Let them practice several times before you begin the story.

Some children will not know the words **bungling** or **botchit**. Explain that bungling is similar to goofing or messing things up. Ask them if they ever had a day when they bungled several things. Tell them you've had a day when you've bungled several things. Tell them you've had days when you mixed up many things. Everyone has days like that. Tell them that another word that means to bungle things is **botch**. Explain that this is a story about a Prince who always botches whatever he does called "Bungling Prince Botchit and the Dangerous Dragon."

Suggestions for Language Development, Discussion, and Creative Activities

Language Development: Sometimes the names of characters in stories hint at things about those characters. Prince Botchit always botches it. Ask your students, "Do these names give you any idea what the characters might be like? Mrs. Goodygood, Mr. Slime, Mayor McPride, Slim Stick, Spot, Midnight the Stallion, Snowflake the Fairy." Have them make up some names that might show characters are mean, honest, always crying, never still, very silly, terribly dumb, a cross between a unicorn and a singer, an alien, and a huge ugly monster.

Art Activity: Ask each student to draw his idea of the most frightening monster he can think of and give it a name. Crayons and white paper will do.

Creative Writing: This story is a fairy tale. A fairy tale is a simple kind of story that deals with supernatural beings such as fairies, ogres, magicians, and dragons. Many times the tale will also have princes, princesses, kings, and queens. Some examples of fairy tales are *Snow White*, *Cinderella*, and *The Three Billy Goats Gruff*. Ask each student to write a simple fairy tale using a fairy, ogre, magician, or dragon.

Game, Tasty Words: The purpose behind this game is to increase vocabulary and encourage the children to use more specific words in order to communicate better. Within a given time period (three minutes is plenty for younger grades), ask your students to name adjectives that describe a taste. "This tastes _____."

Have them get as specific as possible. **Bad** is not as specific as **sour, peppery, spicy, garlicky**. Get them started by suggesting tastes they dislike, then like. Don't forget flavors. Write the words on the chalkboard, listing all that are volunteered.

Dragons

Books:

Custard the Dragon and the Wicked Knight by Ogden Nash. Little Brown, 1961. (Humorous and fun poem turned into a picture book. A personal favorite.)

The Dragon Takes a Wife by Walter Dean Myers. Bobbs-Merrill, 1972. (Delightful and humorous.)

Everyone Knows What a Dragon Looks Like by Jay Williams. Four Winds, 1976. (Beautifully illustrated Chinese story. Perhaps too long for kindergartners.)

The Judge by Margot Zemach. Farrar, Straus, and Giroux, 1969. (Humorous tale.)

There's No Such Thing as a Dragon by Jack Kent. Golden Press, 1976. (Available in record from Western Publishing Company.)

Records:

Pete's Dragon, Walt Disney Productions, 1977. (Also available in a read-along record.)

There's No Such Thing as a Dragon. Western Publishing Company. (A read-along record. Also in book form.)

Songs:

''I Saw a Dragon.'' From the record *Pete's Dragon*. Walt Disney Productions, 1977.

''Puff the Magic Dragon.'' From the record *Children's Greatest Hits*, Volume II, CMS, 1977.

Poems:

''Dragon Night.'' From *Dragon Night and Other Lullabies* by Jane Yolen. Methuen, 1981. (unpaged)

''Us Two.'' From *The Christopher Robin Book of Verse* by A. A. Milne. Dutton, 1967, p. 9.

Filmstrips:

The Judge by Margot Zemach. Miller Brody, 1975. (46 frames.)

Chapter XII

Hopper's Whoppers

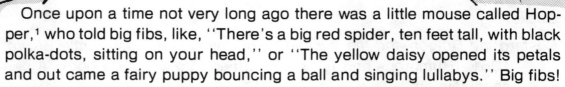

Once upon a time not very long ago there was a little mouse called Hopper,[1] who told big fibs, like, "There's a big red spider, ten feet tall, with black polka-dots, sitting on your head," or "The yellow daisy opened its petals and out came a fairy puppy bouncing a ball and singing lullabys." Big fibs!

Of course no one believed her whoppers, except her little brother Bert.[2] He believed everything she said until one day when the mouse family was picnicking in the clover field.

"Mee-moo. Mee-moo. Mee-moo," chanted Hopper. She had been exploring the creek near the picnic spot. "Mee-moo. Mee-moo."

"What's that noise?" Bert asked.

"It's a sound I heard," Hopper answered mysteriously.

"Where?"

"Well," Hopper said. Her black eyes shone with excitement. "When I was walking near the creek, I saw a spaceship. It was big and round with yellow blinking lights. It was a solar saucer from Mars. And there were little blue mice—and—"

"Really?" said Bert. "Weren't you scared?"

"No, I—"

Before Hopper could say any more, Mother Mouse stopped her.[3] "Hopper!" she said in that don't-say-any-more tone. "Hopper is telling a whopper," Mother said.

"Oh, that so?" Bert said, and he walked away.[4] Now no one wanted to listen to Hopper. Not her mother.[5] Not Uncle Earl. And now, not Bert.[7]

Hopper curled her tail and ate the picnic in silence. If no one will listen to her, she thought, maybe I'll never talk again.

After the meal was over, Mother said, "Go and play but don't go far.[8] But Hopper didn't listen. She walked through the tall grasses.[9] She crossed the little creek. She ran through a cornfield. She heard Uncle Earl calling her to wait, but she didn't.[10]

While she was nibbling some corn, a huge shadow covered the ground.[11] Hopper held very still. Then plop! On top of her dropped a bag closing out the day.[12] Hopper didn't move. Then the bag toppled over, turning her upside down in the bottom. Now she could see the sky out the top.[13] In the sky was the face of a boy. "Hello, little mouse," he said. "You're going to be a birthday present to my friend Tim. Then he closed the paper bag.[14]

Hopper nibbled a tiny hole in the bag. It tasted awful. Now she could see through the hole. They walked a long way down a dusty road. Inside a big iron gate that said **Z O O**, he set the bag on a table.[15] There were many boys and girls wearing party hats and carrying presents. In the background Hopper heard roars and growls, caws and squeals, barks and hoots.

Hopper began to chew on the bitter bag. She chewed a hole almost as big as her head. She saw the boy reaching for the bag. She stuck out her head, and in one powerful hop she ripped through the hole.[16] She ran across the table, climbed down on the bench, and jumped to the ground.[17]

The yelling children grabbed at her, but she was fast. She ran across the cement and up a wall of stones. But she didn't go any farther.

On the other side of the wall was a deep hole. Inside the hole was a cat.[18] Not an ordinary cat—which was terrible enough—but a cat much bigger than a dog—a cat with orange and black stripes. It yawned and showed rows of knife-sharp teeth.

Hopper turned and ran back toward the boys.[19] "There she goes," one shouted as he stamped his foot. His foot caught the tip of her tail, but Hopper pulled and got free. She ran and ran. She ran through some grass, under a bush, and across the dirt. And then she looked up—and up—and up.[20]

Looming over her was a gray, wrinkly animal as big as a car.[21] Its big ears flapped. Its legs were like tree trunks. And it had a fat hose for a nose.

Hopper closed her eyes, waiting for the big animal to step on her.[22] She waited. And she waited. She opened one eye just a crack.[23] Then the other eye.[24] The big animal backed up.[25] Hopper took a step forward,[26] and the big animal turned and ran away. He was scared of Hopper. Hopper ran across the dirt yard[27] while the big animal ran in circles and trumpeted through his big hose.[28]

Hopper raced across the hot cement. Then she squeezed under a bush.[29] She ran down the road, through the cornfield, across the creek, and through the tall grasses until she was safe in the picnic area with her family.[30]

Hopper lay down and puffed for three minutes before she began talking. "I was captured. I was almost eaten by a cat bigger than a dog. And a big gray animal as big as a car was scared of me."

"Hopper's telling a whopper," Bert said pointing at her. "Hopper's telling a whopper."

"But it's true," Hopper said, but no one was listening to her. Hopper said nothing while the family packed up the picnic. They were waiting for Uncle Earl to get back.

Then his deep voice called, "I tried to save her from the boy.[31] He took her to the zoo." Then he saw Hopper. "The tiger didn't eat you. And the elephant didn't trample you!" He ran and hugged Hopper.[32]

Now everyone, especially Bert wanted to listen to Hopper. "Tell us," they all begged.[33]

So Hopper began her true story. She didn't need whoppers any more because she had a real story to tell. And just so no one got mixed up, Hopper promised herself never to tell made-up whoppers, only real stories. Then everyone always would want to listen to Hopper.

Guideline for Telling the Story

The action in this story makes it easy to tell. In addition to the first and last paragraphs, the description of the tiger (right after footnote 18) and the description of the elephant (after 21) should be memorized. Be sure not to use the words **elephant** and **tiger** until Uncle Earl used them near the end of the story.

The spaceship sound, ''Mee-moo,'' should be high-pitched and repetitive. Perhaps before the story begins you can ask the children what a spaceship might sound like; then use their sound in place of ''Mee-moo.''

Near the end of the story Bert taunts, ''Hopper's telling a whopper.'' This should be done in a singsong chant. See Figure 12-1 below for suggested musical tones. This taunt is the part of the story that the children will be repeating for the next week or two.

Figure 12-1 Musical Notation

Hop-per's   telling   a   /   whop-per.

Outline

I. Hopper is a mouse who tells whoppers.
- A. At a picnic she tells Bert about a spaceship.
- B. Mother Mouse stops her.
- C. Hopper pouts.

II. Hopper goes out to play after the picnic.
- A. She won't wait for Uncle Earl.
- B. She is caught by a boy.
- C. The boy takes her to the zoo as a birthday present for his friend.

III. At the zoo she escapes.
- A. The children chase her.
- B. She runs into the cage of a tiger.
- C. She runs into the cage of an elephant.
- D. She runs from the zoo to the family picnic spot.

IV. She tells the story of her adventure.
- A. No one believes her.
- B. Uncle Earl returns and confirms her story.
- C. Now, the family wants to hear her story.

Felt Characters and Props

1. Felt characters: Hopper, Bert, Mother Mouse, Uncle Earl, Tiger, and Elephant.
2. A small paper bag with a bow attached to it. Remember if you need to tell the story more than once, you will need one bag for each telling.
3. Felt board and stand.
4. Text of the story.

Elephant

Tiger

Hopper

Bert

Mother Mouse

Uncle Earl

Movements of the Felt Board Characters

Generally the movements of the felt board characters follow the action of the story. With the six characters and a small paper bag, this tale is easy to tell.

Begin with the felt board empty. At 1 put Hopper in the center of the board. At 2 put Bert next to her. At 3 add Mother Mouse. Move Bert farther away from Hopper at 4. At 5 point to Mother Mouse. At 6 add Uncle Earl. At 7 point to Bert. At 8 take off Mother Mouse and Bert.

When part II begins, Hopper and Uncle Earl are left on the board. At 9 begin to move Hopper progressively away from Uncle Earl. At 10 remove Uncle Earl. At 11 hold a small paper bag over Hopper. At 12 scoop Hopper into the small paper bag leaving the felt board empty. At 13 open the top of the bag and look in. At 14 close the bag. At 15 tear a tiny hole in the bag from the inside. The easiest way to do this is to pinch a little fold and then rip it. It is difficult to poke a hole in a paper bag. At 16 set the bag down on a table. Be sure the top is closed.

As part III begins, the felt board is empty. Hopper is in the bag. The bag is on the table. At 17 rip the bag open from the inside. Stick your hand inside the bag and just rip it open. Push Hopper out, then place her on the felt board. At 18 move Hopper around the board during the action. Add the tiger at 19. At 20 remove the tiger and quickly move Hopper from one side to another as if she were running frantically. Look up and up, as if you are seeing something very tall at 21. Add the elephant at 22. At 23 close your eyes and cringe. At 24 open one eye. At 25 open the other eye. At 26 move the elephant away from Hopper. At 27 move Hopper forward. At 28 run Hopper across the board. At 29 take off the elephant. At 30 begin to move Hopper from place to place. At 31 position Hopper in the center of the board and add Mother Mouse and Bert.

At the beginning of part IV, Hopper, Mother Mouse, and Bert are on the board. At 32 add Uncle Earl. At 33 move Uncle Earl next to Hopper. At 34 arrange Bert, Mother Mouse, and Uncle Earl around Hopper.

Hints

Small children at the kindergarten and first grade level might need the word **whopper** defined. Tell them that **whopper** means very big. Say, ''If I said I caught a **whopper** of a fish, I mean I caught a **big** fish. A **whopper** of a sandwich is a **big** sandwich. A **whopper** of a fib is a **big** lie. This is the story of a mouse who tells big fibs or whoppers.''

Make sure all children know what **z o o** spells. Say, ''You all know that **z o o** spells zoo. Don't you?'' That way even the ones who don't know can say ''Yes.''

Suggestions for Language Development, Discussion, and Creative Activities

Language Development: Have everyone make up some whoppers, either verbally or on paper. The purpose of this activity is to increase imagination and verbal ability.

Language Development: Take turns describing an animal without telling its name like Hopper describes the tiger and elephant. Try a mouse, dog, giraffe, rhinoceros, camel, lion, and deer.

Discussion: Talk about events that sound impossible, sound like whoppers, but are true. For example, Neil Armstrong walked on the moon. Or Dr. Salk discovered an immunization against polio, a disease with no known cure. When Columbus said the world was round, most people thought he was telling a whopper.

Imaginary or Real Game: The leader makes a statement like ''The frog jumped so high he bumped his head on the moon.'' When the leader gives the signal, the children are instructed to stand up and say, ''Imaginary'' if the statement is make-believe or to sit and say, ''Real'' if the statement is possible. Two quieter motions could be substituted for the jumping up and shouting if there is a need to keep the group quiet. This game eases the wiggles of a young group who can't sit very long. It also reinforces the distinction between imagination and reality.

Resources for a Story Hour

Mice

Books:

Whose Mouse Are You? by Robert Kraus. Collier, 1970. (A simple reassuring tale.)

Once a Mouse by Marcia Brown. Scribner, 1961. (An award-winning Indian fable.)

Anatole by Eve Titus. McGraw, 1956. (Fun story of a cheese-tasting French mouse.)

Frederick by Leo Lionni. Pantheon, 1967. (A colorful book about a mouse philosopher.)

Poems:

''Hickory, Dickory, Dock,'' a nursery rhyme. From *Frank Baber's Mother Goose* selected by Ruth Spriggs. Crown, 1976, p. 104.

''Six Little Mice Sat Down to Spin,'' a nursery rhyme. From *Frank Baber's Mother Goose* selected by Ruth Spriggs. Crown, 1976, p. 50.

''The Christening'' by A. A. Milne. From *When We Were Very Young.* Dutton, 1924, p. 5.

''Missing'' by A. A. Milne. From *When We Were Very Young.* Dutton, 1924, p. 52.

''The Dormouse and the Doctor'' by A. A. Milne. From *When We Were Very Young.* Dutton, 1924, p. 66.

''Mice'' by Rose Fyleman. From *Time for Poetry*, compiled by May Hill Arbuthnot. Scott, Foresman, 1959, p. 106.

''Nine Mice'' by Jack Prelutsky. From *The New Kid on the Block*. Greenwillow, 1984, p. 9.